SATAN'

It was mainly to please her father that
Sabina had agreed to marry Nicholas
Freed—but she supposed she would have
been happy enough, if at the last
moment she hadn't met Joel Brent and
fallen deeply in love with him. But what
was the use of dreaming about Joel, who
would never forget the only woman for
him—his dead love Nicole?

SATAN'S MASTER

BY

CAROLE MORTIMER

MILLS & BOON LIMITED
15–16 BROOK'S MEWS
LONDON W1A 1DR

First published 1981
Australian copyright 1981
Philippine copyright 1981
This edition 1981

© Carole Mortimer 1981

ISBN 0 263 73541 9

Set in Monophoto Times 10 on 11½ pt.

*Made and printed in Great Britain by
Richard Clay (The Chaucer Press) Ltd,
Bungay, Suffolk*

LULI
my inspiration

CHAPTER ONE

AT last she was on her way, her legs seeming too short for the bicycle she had hired in Inverness for this holiday of hers. Cycling in Scotland, mainly along the side of the Caledonian Canal, a series of lochs that went from one side of Scotland to the other, had seemed a good idea when she was in London. Now she wasn't so sure.

It was years since she had ridden a bicycle, as she had proved to the man she had hired it from as she wobbled precariously down the road after paying for her two weeks' hire. A couple of her friends had spent their holidays this way last year, at first for a laugh, and then because they were enjoying themselves.

Sabina's father had been horrified when she had told him of her plans to go away for a few days, claiming she couldn't possibly leave London now, not when the wedding was only eight weeks away. Her wedding. To Nicholas Freed, her father's partner in the running of one of the major daily newspapers.

But she had known she had to get away, had to go somewhere where she could collect her thoughts together, decide whether marrying Nicholas was the right thing for her.

She had only hired the bicycle an hour ago and already she was thinking clearer, something she had found impossible to do when in close proximity with her father. He had dominated her all of her nineteen years, made all her decisions for her, including the one that she marry Nicholas.

But Nicholas was of her father's generation, forty-five years of age, with two marriages already behind him. That she had let things get this far, to a four-month engagement and the actual wedding a matter of weeks away, was a source of wonder to Sabina. Not that she didn't like Nicholas, she did, but she wasn't sure she wanted him for a husband. He was attractive enough, tall, slim, dark, with deep blue eyes, and yet she couldn't help wondering what he had done to his second wife to give her grounds for divorcing him. Her father had dismissed her nervousness, saying she wasn't to worry about such things. But then he wasn't the one marrying Nicholas!

Sabina took time out from these depressing thoughts to admire the beautiful scenery all around her. She had left Inverness behind her now, was riding along beside the River Ness, and soon she would see the wonder of the legendary Loch Ness. Her friends had taken this same route last year, and their enthusiasm about the beauty here had made her want to experience it for herself. Crazy, her father had called her yesterday morning when she had left their home with her packed rucksack, and crazy she might be, but she was enjoying herself, was enjoying her first freedom in years.

The sight of a public telephone box, and these thoughts of her father, reminded her that she ought to call him and put his mind at rest about her safety. They only had each other since her mother had died five years ago, and consequently he tended to be more possessive about her than was usual in a father/daughter relationship.

The telephone only rang once before it was snatched up, almost as if he had been sitting next to it waiting for her call. It appeared that he had. 'Where the hell in Scotland are you?' he demanded angrily.

'I'm not silly enough to tell you that,' Sabina said

with a smile. 'If you knew you'd come up here and take me back.'

'Too damned right I would,' he snapped. 'Nicholas is none too happy about your behaviour either.'

'You've told him?'

'I could hardly keep it a secret, you are engaged to the man.'

His sarcasm wasn't lost on her. She sighed. 'You know my reasons for being here, Daddy.'

'Because you need to think! A fine time to start having second thoughts, eight weeks before the wedding. I—— What the hell was that?' he demanded. 'Sabina, are you still there?'

She had put some more money in the box, waiting for the noise of the pips to stop before speaking again. 'Don't panic, Daddy,' she smiled. 'It was just the telephone wanting more money.'

He sighed his impatience. 'Why didn't you reverse the charges? I don't want to be interrupted by that row every couple of minutes.'

'You won't be, because I don't intend putting any more money in. I only called to let you know I haven't been carried away by a rapist or mass murderer.'

'There is no need to mock, Sabina,' he cautioned sternly. 'They do have those sort of things in Scotland too, you know.'

'I'm sure they do,' she agreed dryly. 'But I—— There go the pips again, Daddy. I won't be calling again.'

'Sabina——'

'See you in two weeks' time,' she had time to say before the line was cut off.

She got back on her bicycle, the long length of her legs still golden from the weeks she had spent in Monte Carlo earlier in the summer. Her denim shorts fitted her like a glove, the deep pink tee-shirt moulded to her bare breasts. She made an attractive picture as she cycled down the road that edged Loch Ness, the light breeze lifting her long straight blonde hair off her nape, her green eyes glowing in anticipation of this holiday.

She wasn't surprised at her father's horror at her location, never having been to Scotland himself he couldn't even begin to appreciate the beauty here. It was everything her friends had said it was, peaceful, exhilarating, but most of all breathtakingly beautiful.

For one thing Loch Ness was so large, like a miniature ocean, and she could see one or two motor-cruisers on its length, probably holidaymakers like herself. The banks of the Loch rose steeply either side, a smattering of sheep just visible to her on the luxurious green grass on the other side, the road cut into her side of the Loch before it too rose steeply, one or two cottages just visible in the denseness of the trees.

Because she had picked her bicycle up late in the day it was already well into evening by the time she reached her set destination of the day, Urquhart Castle, the ruins of which overlooked Urquhart Bay. She had a tent and all the necessary equipment for camping, but as there were a couple of hotels in the area she decided to stay at one of them for the night and look the castle over in the morning.

'Morning' was almost lunchtime by the time Sabina emerged from the exhausted sleep she had fallen into as soon as her head touched the downy pillow. When she tried to move, the whole of her body seemed to ache— in places she hadn't even known she could ache! She must be sadly out of condition if a simple bike ride could make her feel this way. But it had been quite a few miles ride, more miles than she had cycled for more years than she could remember.

She hobbled out of bed, a quick bath easing away

some of her aches and pains, deciding to have an early lunch instead of bothering with any breakfast. After all, it was almost twelve o'clock. The day didn't look as warm as yesterday, a light drizzle was falling, a slight mist stopping a clear view of what Sabina knew to be magnificent scenery. Well, she had to look at the ruins of the castle now she was here, might even take a picture of two—if only to prove to her father what a good time she had had.

She donned denims and a sweater. a light waterproof the only clothing she had to keep out the rain. While paying for her bill she asked the proprietor if she could leave her bicycle here while she went down to look at Urquhart Castle.

'You'll not be going far today, I'm thinking,' the middle-aged man took her key.

Sabina smiled. 'I thought I might try and get as far as Fort Augustus.'

He shook his head, frowning darkly. 'I wouldn't recommend you going anywhere, not in this weather.'

Sabina looked down at the light drizzle. 'It doesn't look too bad to me.'

'It never does. But the heavy mist can come down mighty fast. It's a fair trek to Fort Augustus, I wouldn't want you to get lost.'

'But it's a straight road, isn't it?'

'Aye, it's straight,' he nodded. 'But there's tracks leading off the road to the cottages, ye ken, and it's mighty easy to take one of them by mistake.'

'I'll take care,' she promised lightly, pulling her hood over her hair and braving the light rain.

The castle stood in the curve of Urquhart Bay, over-looking Loch Ness in all its glory, although the mist clung to the water like a thin white sheet. The guidebook she had bought in Inverness told her that the castle dated back to the thirteenth century, although improvement had been made during the sixteenth century.

The castle was placed perfectly for watch over Loch Ness, and had obviously been a stronghold for the Scottish Crown in the past. Now all that remained was the square keep, the crumbled ruins of its turret and outer walls. Sabina wandered amongst what must surely have once been a magnificent castle, its splendour still evident in the grey stones that made up its structure.

In the end she decided not to take any photographs now but try and get some on the way back if she could. The last thing she wanted was to show her father pictures of it pouring with rain! And it was pouring now, absolutely bucketing down. She decided to have a coffee in the hotel lounge while she waited for the rain to abate somewhat.

'You're going, then?' the proprietor asked as she made a move about an hour later.

'I thought I would,' she nodded.

He shook his head dourly. 'I think you're making a mistake.'

'If it looks like getting any worse I promise I'll turn around and come back.'

In actual fact that was something she couldn't do, not unless she walked. The front tyre of her bicycle suddenly went flat, and no amount of pumping it up made any difference to its condition, and the mist chose that moment to close in on her like a blanket, making it impossible for her to see farther than a few feet in front of her. There was nothing else for it, she would have to walk, and as she was sure she was nearer to Fort Augustus than Urquhart Castle she decided to go on rather than turn back.

Just where she went wrong she didn't know; all she did know was that the surface of the road didn't feel smooth any more, and groping down on her hands and knees she found that it wasn't the road at all but a roughly cut dirt pathway. Where it led to she couldn't even begin to guess, and she couldn't even see her map in this mist, let alone read it.

If only she had listened to the man at the hotel! He had sounded like a local, had probably lived here all his life, and he obviously knew a lot more about the sudden dropping of the mist than she did.

Well, it was no good standing here berating herself; should she go on or should she attempt to find her way back to the road? One thing groping about on the pathway had told her, there was the mark of hoofprints there, hoofprints going forward, not back. But where would the path take her? She didn't remember seeing a village in this direction when she checked the map this morning.

She sighed. She really had no choice but to go on; she wasn't sure of her way back, and at least she knew there must be some form of habitation in this direction. She only hoped the owner of that habitation wouldn't mind an uninvited guest for the night—she could hardly pitch her tent in this.

Keeping to the roughly hewn pathway didn't prove too difficult; either side of her were tall trees, making it impossible for her to deviate. Nevertheless, she almost felt faint with relief when she saw a glimmer of yellow light in front of her. After almost an hour of this stumbling progress she had been beginning to doubt ever seeing another human being again.

But there had to be humans where there was electric lighting, and as she reached the front of the low, white-painted cottage she saw a spiral of smoke drifting through the lighter coloured mist. Light *and* warmth, it sounded like heaven to Sabina, and reminded her of how damp her clothing had become.

A sharp tap on the door heralded no reaction whatsoever, so she knocked again. Still no answer. There *had* to be someone here. She walked along the front of the cottage to the window with the chink of light showing through, trying to see in through the tiny gap in the curtains. She felt herself tense as the curtains moved slightly, two venomous green eyes suddenly appearing in front of her and making her let out a bloodcurdling scream.

'Satan's no more enthusiastic about nosey-parkers than I am,' remarked a cold voice from behind her.

Sabina swung round to see the owner of that unwelcoming voice. Standing in front of her, the mist swirling eerily about him, stood a tall dark man dressed completely in black—black cords and black jumper, his hair also jet black, long and unkempt. His face was gaunt, all strong angles, the focal point being a pair of cold grey eyes that remained unblinkingly on her white face. He was a handsome man in a pagan sort of way, the handsomest man Sabina had ever seen.

'Wh—who are you?' her voice quivered.

His mouth twisted tauntingly. 'I'm Satan's master, who else?'

Sabina woke to find herself lying on a sofa, the hardest article of furniture she had ever sat on in her life. She had never fainted before either, for that was surely what had happened. God, that man—Satan's master! She swung her legs to the floor, sitting up to come face to face with him.

He turned from his morose study of the fire, a man possibly in his late thirties, his expression not lightening as he saw her looking at him with wide frightened eyes. 'So you've decided to wake up, have you?' he rasped, pushing the black cat off his lap and standing up. 'Who are you?' he demanded. 'And what are you doing here?'

Sabina's mouth felt dry. 'I—er—I asked you first,' she said with a return of her usual spirit.

'And I told you,' he replied sharply, his voice deep and husky.

'Of course you didn't,' she said with a nervous laugh. She had behaved stupidly a few minutes ago; this man might be dark and frightening, but he certainly had no connection with the devil. 'That cat is Satan, isn't he?'

'He is.'

'And you're his owner.'

White teeth showed in the glimmer of a smile. 'No one owns Satan. He just goes with the cottage. The locals believe the previous owner, a certain Mrs McFee, was a witch.'

'That's ridiculous!'

His steady gaze remained levelled on her. 'Is it?'

Sabina swallowed hard. 'You know it is.'

'Do I?'

'Of course it is! No rational human being——'

His dark eyebrows rose, straight black brows that disappeared into the untidy swathe of dark hair that fell over his forehead. There was something about this man, something familiar . . . 'Who says I'm a rational human being?' his soft attractive voice taunted. 'Who says I'm even human?'

'Stop teasing me!' She pushed back the hood that had been hiding her hair, unzipping her anorak. 'Would you mind if I took this off?' she indicated the damp garment.

'Take off anything you want,' he invited, already insolently appraising the curves she had revealed. 'Female company has been in short supply around here.'

Sabina blushed under his intent stare, and left her

coat on, wanting to wrap her arms protectively about her as he continued to look at her. 'Then why do you live here?' she snapped angrily. Her first impression of this man being a ghostly figure was completely wrong, he was all too human, despite his casting doubts upon the fact minutes earlier.

His face hardened, the angles sharper than ever, his eyes glacial. 'I live here because it suits me to. Now I repeat, who are you?'

'Sabina—Sabina Smith.' She couldn't stop looking at him, there was something so familiar about him, something at the back of her mind telling her she should know him, or someone like him. Without the dark growth of two or three days' beard he would be——

'What are you staring at?' He kicked viciously at one of the logs burning in the fire, sending sparks all over the hearth. 'Well?' he demanded. 'Answer me!'

'I—I—— You——'

'Yes?' His eyes bored into hers, holding her immobile.

'You remind me of someone,' she said nervously, the anger about that firm sensuous mouth making her cower in her seat.

He stepped forward, his hands biting painfully into her upper arms as he wrenched her to her feet. 'Who?' His face was only inches from hers as he shook her. 'Who do I remind you of?' he repeated.

'I—I don't know.' She was beginning to feel faint— for the second time today. 'I don't know,' she cried, tears gathering in her distressed green eyes. 'What sort of man are you, to treat me like this? Let me go. Let me go, I tell you!'

His teeth bared viciously. 'Not until you answer me. So tell me, who do I remind you of?'

Right at this moment he reminded her of the devil

she had first thought him, the skin stretched tautly
across his hollow cheeks, shadows beneath his cold grey
eyes. But that growth of beard was completely human,
although it made him more satanic than ever.

Sabina took a step backwards, unwittingly stepping
on the cat's paw. The same paw snaked out and caught
her a savage blow on the ankle, as the cat growled its
displeasure before running up the wooden staircase that
led to the top floor of the cottage.

She winced. 'Your cat shares your dislike of my being
here.' Her ankle felt sore already, and she was sure she
could feel blood trickling down on to her foot. 'I——
Could I just see to my ankle?' she asked her captor.

'Why not?' He thrust her away from him. 'And you're
right, Satan speaks for both of us. I don't want you
here, Miss Smith, for any reason,' he added grimly.

Sabina was once again sitting on the lumpy sofa, the
rest of the furniture and threadbare carpet in just as
deplorable a condition. And yet the man's clothes
looked of good quality. He was a complete mystery, an
enigma who wanted her out of his life as quickly as she
had come into it.

'Has the mist cleared?' The scratch on her ankle was
red and sore-looking, the blood flowing freely. She took
out a tissue to staunch the flow, her long blonde hair
escaping the collar of her anorak and falling down over
her face.

'No.' He was looking at her with narrowed watchful
eyes.

'Then you can't expect me to go out in that again,'
she said in disbelief, pushing her straight hair back
behind her ears.

'I didn't exactly say that, only that I don't want you
here.'

'I'd never find my way back to the road,' she insisted.

He shrugged. 'You found your way here, you could go back the same way.' He turned to stare morosely into the fire.

Sabina racked her brains to think where she had seen that face before—although not exactly that face. This stranger was too thin, his features too harsh, the hair too long and out of style. She jumped nervously as hard grey eyes turned to look at her.

'Well?' he rasped.

'I didn't find my way here, I got lost,' she snapped. 'Now do you have some antiseptic I might put on this?' she indicated her ankle. 'Your *pet* has hurt me.'

'And so will I if you stay here.' His voice was harsh. 'So you stay and take the consequences.'

'C-consequences?' she quavered.

'There's only one bedroom,' he drawled tauntingly.

'So? I—I can sleep down here on the sofa.' Although how she would sleep on all those lumps was beyond her. 'I won't be any trouble, Mr—er—really I won't. If I could just stay here until the mist clears . . .'

The intentness of his gaze unnerved her even more than she was already. 'Sometimes that takes days,' he informed her.

'D-days?'

'That's right,' he nodded. 'How will you like being stuck here with me for days, with no one to help you?'

'Would I need help?' Sabina threw her head back in challenge.

'You might,' he said tightly, his eyes on the golden blondeness of her hair.

'From you?' She was curiously breathless at the prospect.

'From me,' he nodded, his gaze still fixed on her hair. 'I told you, women haven't been too plentiful around here. I've been here almost a year now, and no woman has crossed that threshhold until today. If you doubt my masculinity . . .' he lunged forward and pulled her ruthlessly to her feet, bending his head to grind his mouth down savagely on hers.

After her initial resistance Sabina felt herself begin to weaken, felt his hands move beneath her anorak, pulling up her jumper to mould her breasts in the palms of his hands, his thumbs teasing her nipples into throbbing life. She recoiled in shock, straightening her clothing as she backed away from him.

His face had darkened with cruel humour. 'What's the matter, *Miss Smith*?' he taunted. 'I thought someone like you would do anything for a story.'

'Someone like me?' she repeated dazedly, her senses still reeling from his onslaught. 'And for what story?'

'Oh, come on, *Miss Smith*, you know exactly what I mean.'

Sabina frowned. 'Why do you keep saying my name like that, almost accusingly?'

'Because I am accusing you, damn you,' he was furiously angry now, the eyes she had thought cold burning with fierce anger. 'I'm accusing you of coming here to spy on me, of using every trick you can think of to get me to talk, of——'

'Please,' she put up a resisting hand, very pale. 'Don't say any more. You're wrong about me,' she said shakily. 'I don't even know who you are, let alone what you're trying to hide.'

'I'm not trying to *hide* anything! I'm just sick to death of reporters—nosy, prying reporters who keep trying to twist everything that happened,' his expression was bleak.

Sabina shook her head. 'I'm not a reporter! Whatever gave you the idea I was?'

'You aren't a very good actress, and you could have

tried a more original name than Smith,' he scorned.

'But that is my name,' she insisted. 'I can prove it to you.' She moved to the door.

His hand snaked out and caught her around the wrist. 'Where do you think you're going?'

'To the saddlebags on my bicycle. I—I have identification there.'

'I'll bet you do. And I'll also lay odds on you running like hell once you set foot outside that door. What's the matter, *Miss Smith*, have you decided you can't go through with it, that simply publicising confirmation of my whereabouts will be enough?'

'I don't know what you mean,' she shook her head. 'Go through with what?'

'Oh, I'm sure it all seemed so logical back in London,' he sneered. 'Someone tipped you off on my possible whereabouts and you decided to come up here and get the inside story, literally.'

'Literally?' She trembled as his hold tightened.

'Literally,' he nodded. 'As inside my bed.'

'Inside your——! My God,' she gasped, 'you have a nerve!'

'I have several hundred, and at the moment all of them are attuned to you. Your newspaper chose well, Sabina—I take it that at least that part of your name is true?'

'All of it's true,' she said desperately.

He gave her a scathing look. 'Your cover is blown, Sabina. It was blown the moment I saw your hair and those wide innocent eyes, so you might as well drop the act. You never know, if you play your cards right I could just give you that story after all.' His hand moved up to touch the silkiness of her hair. 'Yes, your editor chose well. I've always had a weakness for blondes.' Once again his head lowered and he claimed her lips, gently this time, parting them persuasively as he deepened the kiss.

In that moment everything in Sabina's life suddenly changed, became more ordered. This man's lips searching and probing hers made any more thoughts of marrying Nicholas unnecessary. She couldn't marry him now. A stranger, a cold hard man embittered by she didn't know what, was making her his with the touch of his lips and hands, was arousing her as no other man ever had, and she couldn't possibly marry anyone else but him.

Her body arched against his, her curves fitting perfectly against the hardness of his body, her hands going up about his shoulders and tangling in the thick blackness of his hair as she strained him closer to her. Whoever he was, whatever he had done to merit being hounded by reporters, she had fallen in love with him.

But although she wasn't a reporter herself, and she might eventually get him to believe that, her father did own and publish a daily newspaper, a newspaper that thrived on scandal. She had nothing in her favour to endear her to this man, and the realisation made her stiffen in his arms.

At once she was set free, grey eyes gleaming down at her in triumph. 'Changed your mind again?' he taunted.

Sabina was still dazed by her recent discovery, sure that things like this didn't happen in real life. It wasn't possible to fall in love with a complete stranger. Why, she didn't even know his name! Her father would dismiss it as a flight of fancy, and perhaps that was what it was, perhaps she had a fever from getting so wet.

'Well, have you?' His stance was challenging.

'I—— No.'

His gaze swept over her with cool mockery, lingering on her bruised and throbbing lips. 'Your body wasn't saying no just now. And neither was mine, as I'm sure you know. I'm also sure you very rarely say no,' he added insultingly.

Colour flooded her cheeks, resentment flared in her eyes. 'Why, you——'

'Which scandal sheet do you work for, Sabina?'

She shook her head. 'I——'

'Which one? The *Chronicle*, *News and Views*, or could it be the worst one of all, the *Daily News*?'

Her face paled as he mentioned her father's newspaper. She knew it was a terrible newspaper, preying on other people's mistakes and misery.

'The *Daily News*,' her tormentor repeated with distaste. 'God, that's really sinking low! And doesn't he mind you using your body as well as your mind to get a story?'

Sabina frowned. 'He?'

His hand came out and pulled on the slender gold chain about her throat, tugging it out of the neckline of her jumper to reveal the ring threaded on its length, the huge diamond flanked by two smaller emeralds. It was her engagement ring, the ring that had been on her finger for the past four months, until yesterday morning when she had decided such a ring was rather conspicuous for the quiet holiday she had intended taking. *Had* being the operative word; meeting this man had changed all that.

'I discovered this during our—encounter, just now,' his mouth twisted. 'And I repeat, doesn't he mind who you sleep with?'

Sabina blushed, remembering where his hand had strayed to discover the ring as it lay nestled between the firm swell of her breasts. 'There's nothing *to* mind,' she dismissed impatiently. 'I'm on holiday——'

'Oh yes?' he scorned.

'Yes,' she flashed.

'Are you also on holiday from him?'

'I'm alone, if that's what you mean.' She instantly wished she hadn't told him that, it made her too vulnerable.

'It wasn't, but thanks for the information.'

'Then what did you mean?'

'I mean is it your usual practice to forget your engagement when it suits you to, when you have another man in your sights?'

Sabins flushed. 'You aren't "in my sights"!' How could she have imagined herself in love with such an insulting, arrogant man! Thank God that madness had passed, leaving only disgust with herself for having responded to him. It must have been the sensual aura he emitted without even being aware of it, that air of sexual excitement about him, that had made her forget all sensibility.

He raised his eyebrows. 'Not even professionally?'

Sabina sighed. 'Well, as I don't even know who you are I can't really say.'

His face darkened, his mouth tight. 'I've already told you to drop the act!'

'I'm sorry it it hurts your ego,' she scorned, 'but I really have no idea of your identity. Are you a bank robber or something?'

'Or something,' he agreed moodily.

'Well, Mr Whoever-you-are, do you have some antiseptic for my ankle?' It was starting to throb now, the cat having curled its claws into her skin before ripping them out again. 'That animal may not have been clean,' she snapped.

'Satan is very clean, all cats are.'

'Nevertheless . . .' she eyed him expectantly.

He turned impatiently on his heel, going through a

door into what looked like a kitchen, a small cramped room that looked barely big enough for the width and height of him. He seemed to be searching through a cabinet over the sink, finally coming back and thrusting a tube of antiseptic at her.

'Thank you,' she accepted quietly, applying the cream to her slender ankle, aware that he watched her every move. She handed the tube back to him. 'Can I leave now?' she asked nervously, suddenly aware that his 'or something' could be the rapist or murderer she had kidded her father about yesterday.

'If you leave where would you go?' His grey eyes were narrowed and watchful.

'I—I have a tent. I suppose I could pitch that some-where.'

He shook his head. 'I'm willing to give you the benefit of the doubt—for the moment. You can stay here tonight.'

'But you said—you said you had no room for me.'

'I said there was only one bed,' he corrected mock-ingly.

'Oh,' she blushed.

'Do you also have a sleeping bag in that seemingly bottomless saddlebag?'

'Yes,' she frowned her puzzlement.

'Then you can share my bed—in the safe cocoon of your sleeping bag, of course.'

'Oh no, I—I'd rather sleep down here on the sofa. If you don't mind.'

'Oh, but I do mind. I can't have a guest of mine sleeping on the sofa,' his words taunted her.

'Then couldn't you——'

'No, I could not! For one thing the sofa isn't long enough for either of us to sleep on, for another thing it's *my* bed. And I'm not willing to put myself out that much for someone I didn't even invite here.'

'I've said I'll go——'

'I wouldn't even send a dog out in that mist. And although reporters are the lowest form of life to me I can't be sure that you are one. But I can't be sure you aren't either,' his voice hardened. 'So tonight you'll stay with me, where I can keep an eye on you.'

Sabina gulped, her eyes wide. 'K-keep an eye on me?'

'I'm still not sure about you, Miss Smith,' he managed to put a wealth of sarcasm into his voice. 'So I'm not leaving you down here where you could snoop about.'

'I don't want to "snoop about" anywhere,' she denied angrily. 'I wouldn't have bothered you at all if I hadn't been lost and it's pouring down with rain.'

'Can you cook?' he asked suddenly.

She frowned. 'Cook?'

'Mm,' her reluctant host nodded. 'Before I came here I had never felt the necessity to learn to cook. Since my arrival here I've had to learn the hard way. Even Satan wouldn't touch some of my earlier efforts.'

'You want *me* to cook you a meal?'

'That was the general idea.'

'Why, you——'

'What's the matter, can't you cook either?'

'Of course I can cook, but——'

'Good.' He sat down in the fireside chair, his long legs stretched out in front of him. 'You'll find the makings of a meal out in the kitchen.'

'You really expect me to cook for you?'

He turned from his contemplation of the fire. 'Is that too much to ask for your board?'

'Well—no, I suppose not,' but her look was resentful.

'Well then?' he raised his eyebrows.

'Okay, *okay*!' She slammed angrily into the kitchen, only to have the door open again seconds later, her dark tormentor standing there. 'What's the matter now?' she challenged. 'Have you come to make sure I don't poison you? There isn't much I could do wrong with bacon and eggs,' she dismissed tautly. 'Even you couldn't ruin them.'

'Maybe not,' he conceded. 'But if there's a woman around I don't see why I should do the work.'

'Oh, I see.' Sabina slammed the ancient frying pan down on the even more ancient electric cooker. 'You believe a woman's place is in the kitchen,' she derided.

'Or the bedroom,' he mocked. 'But that can come later. I just came to tell you that I've brought in your saddlebags, so don't try escaping out of the back door.'

'I wasn't going to. I'm hungry too.' It seemed like years ago, not hours, since she had eaten that early lunch at the hotel.

'For food or love?' he asked huskily, watching the rise and fall of her breasts.

'Food!' she angrily turned her back on him.

'Shame.' He sounded amused. 'I would willingly have forgone my food to have satisfied my other appetite. At the moment I think that one is more in need. A year is a long time to go without a woman.'

'For a man like you I'm sure it is,' Sabina snapped waspishly.

His fingers clamped about her wrist, pulling her round to face him, very close in the confines of the dimly lit kitchen. 'A man like me?' he ground out.

'Well, I—— You—you're obviously a very virile man.'

'Oh yes,' he breathed huskily, 'I'm virile. At the moment, very much so.'

She knew that, his body hard against hers, his thighs leaping with desire. 'Could I get on with the cooking now?' She was too aware of his sensual mouth on a level with her eyes, of the way her body was reacting to his.

He instantly released her. 'Go ahead. You'll have to excuse my keeping touching you—I've been away from a beautiful woman too long.'

'Why—I'm sorry,' she said hastily as his expression darkened. 'I—I won't ask again.'

'Make sure you don't,' he snapped, leaving her.

Dinner was a quiet affair, Sabina wrapped up in her own thoughts, her host seeming to be the same. Satan had appeared halfway through the meal, sitting patiently on a third chair about the old-fashioned table, those slitted green eyes watching every morsel of food that entered their mouths.

'Doesn't he have his own food?' Sabina was beginning to feel uncomfortable under that watchful stare, especially as the cat seemed to resent her eating the food.

Her host patted the black cat, tickling it behind the ears. A loud purr sounded in the silence. 'Of course he has his own food, he just prefers ours. You're almost human, aren't you, boy?'

Quite frankly the black cat frightened Sabina, not because of its size, in fact it was only a small cat compared to some she had seen, but because of the venom in its green eyes every time it looked at her, a look almost of jealousy.

Once again she felt tired; the walk in the mist and rain after her bicycle tyre went flat had made her feel more exhausted than she had the previous evening. But she didn't want this man to know how tired she was, didn't want him to suggest that they go upstairs and share that bed.

'I've put your gear upstairs,' he remarked as if reading her thoughts.

'My bicycle has a puncture.' She hastily spoke of something else.

He nodded. 'I'll take a look at that tomorrow, if the mist clears.'

'Are we far from the road here?'

'Thinking of walking?'

She shrugged. 'If my bicycle can't be mended I just may have to.'

'We're about two miles from the road you left.'

'Only two miles?' she gasped. 'But it took me hours!'

'And it exhausted you.' He stood up. 'Time for bed.'

'No!' Panic filled her. 'I mean—I—I'm really not tired.'

'Liar!' he said softly. 'Your eyelids have been drooping for the past hour. Come on,' he put out a hand to pull her to her feet, 'a good night's sleep will do you good.'

That was the last thing she would get, spending the night with this man. He had already shown her, more than once, that her type of beauty appealed to him—'a weakness for blondes', he had called it. And she had no guarantee he wouldn't try to make love to her, not when he had apparently denied himself female company for so long. She had no guarantee she would be able to deny him either.

She ignored his outstretched hand. 'I'm not sleepy yet. You go up. I—I'll join you later.'

'No fear, little lady.' He bent down and swung her up into his arms. 'You just may be an innocent holiday-maker, but then again you might be a reporter, and until I've made my mind up either way, where I go you go, and vice versa.'

'Everywhere?' Her arms clung around his neck of their own volition, even more aware of the magnetic attraction he held for her this close to him. He didn't smell of body lotion or aftershave as Nicholas did, he smelt of good honest sweat, and an even more basic smell, a male smell that excited and aroused her. His eyes darkened as he looked at her, as if he were aware of the disturbed state of her emotions. Consequently her next words came out sharply, almost defensively. 'I take it this cottage does have somewhere I can wash and—and change into my nightclothes?'

'Oh yes,' he smiled at her bad humour. 'That's why there's only one bedroom. I had the other converted into a bathroom.'

'How nice!' She hoped her sarcasm wasn't lost on him. She could tell by the tightening of his beautifully shaped mouth that it wasn't.

'Be glad that I did,' he rasped. 'Otherwise you might find yourself sitting in an iron tub before the fire right now.'

Sabina gasped, and held her tongue, knowing that she was pushing him to the borderline of his temper.

He carried her up the narrow stairway, kicking open the wooden door directly opposite the top of the stairs, dropping her down on to the bed before turning to switch on the lamp next to the bed. Not that this small light made a lot of difference to the visibility in the room; her host appeared more menacing than ever.

She gave a startled gasp as something touched her hand, turning to see Satan curled up on her sleeping bag. She moved hurriedly away in case the cat struck out at her for the second time today. 'I hope you'll get him off there before I get back,'

'Get back from where?' he raised his eyebrows.

Sabina got her pyjamas out of her saddlebag. 'I'm going to the bathroom,' she informed him crossly. 'And I don't want to have to fight your cat for my part of the bed.' Goodness knows it was going to be bad enough sleeping there without that!

'Don't worry,' he taunted. 'I'd rather have you share

my bed any day—or night.'

She fled, her face bright red with embarrassment. This was terrible, stuck here in the middle of nowhere with a man she didn't even know the name of, a man who feared reporters. No, feared was the wrong word, he despised them, hated them. But why? Why did he——

'Miss Smith?' A loud knock sounded on the door behind her. 'I want to use the bathroom, so unless you want to share that with me too, I should hurry up and get out of there.'

She had already noted that there was no lock on the door, so she quickly put on her pyjamas, glad that she had brought something serviceable rather than one of the glamorous nightgowns she usually wore at home. Her host was standing outside the door when she emerged, his amusement at her masculine attire obvious. Sabina put her head proudly in the air and walked past him.

Her sleeping bag lay on top of the bedclothes, the vicious Satan fortunately removed, so she crawled into its warm covering. A fire had been lit in the grate during her absence, and already the room was beginning to feel warmer. It would have been quite cosy if it wasn't for the fact that she had to share the accommodation with that dangerous man—dangerous to her senses, that was.

She tensed as he came back into the room, silently pulling off the sweater to reveal his naked chest. His hands moved to the buckle of the belt to his cords, looking up to meet her mesmerised eyes as she watched him over the top of her sleeping bag.

'I don't mind providing you with a strip show,' he drawled. 'I'm certainly not ashamed to show my body, but if you're as innocent as you pretend to be then you just might be embarrassed when I take my clothes off.'

Sabina gulped. 'All of them?'

'Isn't that the usual practice when you go to bed?'

'I—— Yes, but—— Yes.' She hurriedly turned away. 'But you'll be putting pyjamas on, won't you?' She heard the cords drop on to the chair beside his sweater.

The bed gave beside her. 'I never wear them.' His voice was close to her ear.

'Oh!' She kept her head turned away, unsure of just how near he was. 'Good—goodnight, Mr—er—goodnight.'

The light went out, only the fire glow to lighten the darkness now. 'Goodnight, Sabina.' He seemed to be settling down under the bedclothes. 'Warm enough?'

'Yes, thank you,' and surprisingly she was.

'That's a shame.' Once again he sounded amused at her expense. 'I could have offered to keep you warm,' he explained his humour.

'That won't be necessary.' Her voice was stilted, her body taut.

'I didn't think so. And no nocturnal wanderings,' he warned harshly. 'Satan might not like it.'

'He wouldn't?' she said nervously.

'No. He's lying in the doorway, as he does every night. And he won't let anyone in or out of this room, unless it's me.'

'He sounds more like a guard dog than a cat,' Sabina snapped moodily, her back firmly turned towards the man lying next to her.

'I think that's exactly what he was for Mrs McFee. She trained him to do that. Now he guards me as well as he did her.'

'In that case, I won't move.'

'Oh, you can move,' she could hear him smile, 'as long as it's in my direction.'

'Goodnight!' she said firmly.

His mocking laughter had her fists clenched at her

sides, but she willed herself not to speak again. She just wanted to fall asleep, get this night over with as quickly as possible, and tomorrow get as far away from this man as she could.

Falling asleep wasn't as easy as it should have been considering her exhaustion, although the deep even breathing of the man at her side soon told her that he had no trouble doing so. She slowly turned to face him, not used to sleeping lying on her right side. He was lying on his back, his arm flung across his eyes, his chest golden in the glow from the fire. He had said he wasn't ashamed of his body, and that wasn't surprising; his flesh was lean and muscular, although she felt sure he was at least in his mid-thirties, a time when most men were worrying about running to fat. This man had no worries in that direction.

'Seen enough?' he murmured suddenly, moving his arm from over his eyes to look at her.

Colour flooded into her cheeks, her eyes were wide with shame. 'I——'

'Because I can always take off all the bedclothes if you haven't,' he taunted.

Oh, she was so embarrassed at being caught looking at him like this. 'I—I——' The colour drained from her face as quickly as it had come into it, her eyes widening with sudden recognition. He had taken advantage of his time in the bathroom to shave the growth of beard from his face, revealing a deep cleft in the centre of his chin, the firmness of his jaw.

He sat up, bending over her. 'What is it?' he demanded sharply, those now familiar grey eyes narrowed. 'Tell me what's wrong,' he ordered savagely.

'I—' she gulped, unable to believe she was really seeing this man. 'You—you're——'

His shoulders stiffened, a harsh light in his eyes. 'You

know, don't you? You know who I am!'

Yes, she knew. His name was Joel Brent. He was a superstar, a singer who ranked up at the top with the Sinatras and the Mathises of this world, legends in their own lifetime. He was a man who had crashed the car he was driving when his girl-friend, Nicole Dupont, had told him she was leaving him for another man. Rumour had it that both of them had been intended to die, Joel Brent's intention being to kill Nicole if he couldn't have her. Only they hadn't both died, only Nicole Dupont had been killed, and Joel Brent had faced a barrage of publicity about whether the crash had been deliberate or merely the accident it appeared to be. Nicole Dupont had always said that Joel was a possessive man, that he would never let go what he thought was his. But as there had been no evidence to confirm that he had intentionally crashed, his name was finally cleared of all blame.

A few weeks later Joel Brent had disappeared, seemingly off the face of the earth. And now Sabina had run into him in a remote Scottish cottage, a man who might have been responsible for deliberately taking Nicole Dupont's life!

CHAPTER TWO

SHE had been staring at him for the last few minutes, unable to believe the evidence of her own eyes. Joel Brent, a man who oozed sex-appeal, whose husky voice seduced every woman who listened to him sing, a man always in demand by the eager public, his sales in records reaching the millions, was lying here on this bed beside her.

She knew a little about him, knew that he was thirty-four, came from somewhere in Hampshire, that Nicole Dupont had been his girl-friend for six months before the accident that had killed her, and that he had no close family, although she doubted he was ever alone.

But he was alone here! Why had he come to such a place? Could it be guilt about Nicole Dupont that had prompted this need for solitude, or could it be that he found life so difficult without the woman he loved that he had chosen to cut himself off from all other humanity?

Sabina looked at the strength in his face, the bitterness, and knew that he felt guilty about nothing, and that strength would never allow him to give in to any weakness. 'You didn't do it,' she said with certainty.

He seemed to tense. 'What did you say?' His voice was low, dangerously so.

Why hadn't she recognised that attractive quality in his voice, that deep timbre that spoke of voice control? She moved uncomfortably as she realised he was waiting for an answer. Her words had been more of a thought, and not meant for him to hear. She bit her lip. 'I said——'

'I know what you said!' He sprang into action, looming over her, his hands trapping her in the confines of the sleeping bag. 'What did you mean by it?'

Sabina eyed him apprehensively. He might not be capable of murder, but he was capable of violence. 'I just meant—— That crash—— You didn't——'

'No, I didn't!' he cut in savagely, his eyes like chips of ice. 'But I didn't need you to tell me that. The subject was covered pretty comprehensively in the newspapers. Of course, no one bothered to ask for my version of what happened, but then the truth might not have made such interesting reading. Has your editor decided it might be a good angle after all?' he asked angrily. 'After a year someone actually wants to know the truth?'

She wished he wasn't quite so close, wished she could at least move her arms, but she lay there trapped beneath him, his bare chest only inches above her, his warm breath caressing her cheek. 'Why didn't you ever tell anyone the truth?' she queried breathlessly, no doubt in her mind that whatever had happened in that crash it had not been Joel Brent's fault.

'Because no one asked me for it,' he snapped. 'And you've just made the biggest mistake of your life, little lady.'

'Wh-what do you mean?'

He smiled, a smile that was mainly cruelty. 'I mean I'd more or less decided to let you leave here in the morning.' His mouth quirked. 'I fell for that innocent look in your huge green eyes,' his hand moved to touch her gently, causing her long lashes to flutter nervously. 'You're ideal for a reporter, Sabina Smith, you have the hair and face of an angel. An impression that's totally deceptive.'

'I'm not a reporter, Mr Brent. Please believe me,' she pleaded.

His harshness remained. 'Who knows,' he spoke softly to himself, 'I might get to like having you around,' his hand smoothed the hair back from her temple, moving to cup her cheek. 'Yes, I think I could get to like it very much.'

'But I—I'll be leaving tomorrow.'

'*Would* have been leaving tomorrow,' he corrected. 'But not now, not when you know who I am, and would very much like to know what I'm doing here.' He flicked the ring as it lay against her partly revealed breasts. 'He'll have to learn to do without you for a while. At the moment my need is greater than his.'

Sabina swallowed hard. 'What do you mean?'

Joel Brent swung away from her, laughing softly. 'Not what you think I mean—not yet anyway. But you see I happen to like living here, and I'm not ready to move on. So for the moment you stay with me.'

'Stay here?' Sabina sat up to look at him, looking away again as she saw the bedclothes had almost fallen back to his hips, revealing his flat, taut stomach. 'I can't stay here,' she protested. 'I'm getting married in eight weeks' time.'

'Are you now?' Joel got out of bed, moving to pull on his cords. 'Now that is interesting.'

Sabina turned around just in time to see him zipping up his trousers. 'Why is it interesting?' Thank God it was dark in here! This man seemed to care nothing for the fact that he was walking around half naked. Oh she had seen men wearing less at the beach, but the confines of this bedroom could hardly be classed in the same light. Although Nicholas had often pressurised for a closer relationship between them she had always refused.

'Who's the lucky man?' He ignored her question.

'Um—his name is—er—Nicholas.'

His eyes narrowed with suspicion. 'Nicholas what?'

'Er—' she shrugged. 'Does it matter?' She would only be damning herself more by revealing who Nicholas really was.

'It didn't,' Joel Brent said slowly. 'Not until you tried to avoid telling me. Hmm,' he gave her a studied look, his head tilted to one side. 'Let's look at this logically. You have an engagement ring with a diamond the size of an ice-cube, you work for the *Daily News*, and you're engaged to a man called Nicholas. Putting all that together I come up with—Nicholas Freed!' He seemed to pounce on her, crossing quickly to the bed and wrenching her chin round to look at him. Her high colour told him what he wanted to know. 'Well, well, well,' he drawled tauntingly. 'What some girls will do to get to the top!'

Her colour deepened. 'It isn't like that! I——'

'How did you get him to propose marriage to you?' he mocked. 'That isn't his style at all. Did you hold back this lovely little body of yours until he waved a wedding ring in front of your nose?' His hands were roughly caressing the hollows of her throat.

'No, of course not! He——'

Joel flung her away from him in disgust. 'You mean you've let him make love to you?' he said with distaste, rubbing his hands down his cords as if the touch of her revolted him. 'Good God, the man must be at least thirty years older than you.'

'Twenty-six,' she corrected huskily. 'I'm nineteen.'

'And he's *forty-five*? It's disgusting!'

Sabina swallowed hard. 'I'm sorry you feel that way. Actually, I—I'm not going to marry him now, I've changed my mind.'

'Why?' he sneered. 'Couldn't you take the weekly beatings you would be expected to endure?'

Her face was white, her eyes huge. 'B-beatings?'

Joel Brent gave a harsh laugh. 'Don't tell me he hasn't hit you yet? His second wife couldn't take those beatings, but perhaps you're one of those women who enjoy that sort of thing.'

'Of course I'm not! Do you know Nancy Freed?'

'Yes, I know her.'

'And Nicholas used to—he used to hit her?' She couldn't believe it. Surely her father must have known of this too. How could he let her marry a man like that?

'He *beat* her,' Joel corrected grimly. 'Although she said she'd fallen over.'

'Maybe she had,' Sabina said hopefully.

'She didn't,' he said with certainty.

Sabina felt sick. 'I didn't know.' Her voice was faint.

'Maybe not,' he shrugged. 'You could only have been nine or ten at the time they separated.'

Then her father *had* known, he had been Nicholas' partner for the last fifteen years. And he had been going to let her marry such a monster. But why? It was a question only he could answer. 'Do you have a telephone?' she asked Joel Brent.

'Why?' His eyes were narrowed.

'I—I need to call someone.'

He shook his head. 'Not from here you won't. I don't have a telephone, radio, television, or read newspapers.'

So that was why he didn't know she was Charles Smith's daughter, why he took her to just be a young reporter taking the easy way to the top of her career. How wrong could he be! She had never worked in her life, a little charity work was as near as she had ever come to it. Her father always said he needed her at home whenever she suggested going out to work, and Nicholas seemed to feel the same way when she had told him she would like to get a job after they were married. Maybe if she had had a job, had gained a little independence from her father, she might not have been so easily persuaded to marry Nicholas.

'Then you don't know that the public are anxious to know what's happened to you?' she now asked Joel Brent.

He seemed to stiffen. 'They were quick enough to condemn me a year ago.'

'But——'

'I don't conduct interviews at two o'clock in the morning, Miss Smith,' he cut in harshly. 'In fact I don't conduct interviews at all, not any more.'

'I was only——'

'I don't care what you were only!' His face was livid with anger. 'You can sleep in this bed tonight, tomorrow we'll have to try and fix up some other arrangement.'

'T-tomorrow?' she queried.

'I've already told you, you aren't leaving, not until I do. And that may not be for months yet.'

'But I just told you I can't stay here! Mr Brent, I——'

'Joel!' he snapped. 'If you have to call me anything call me Joel. I don't get many visitors, just the occasional neighbour, and they have no idea that my name is Brent. Do you understand?'

'Yes. But—— Where are you going?' Her question stopped him going out of the door.

'What's the matter, aren't you used to sleeping alone?'

'I always sleep alone!' she told him through gritted teeth.

'Always?' he taunted.

'Yes!'

'I wonder if Freed has ever taken a virgin?' he mused cruelly. 'I doubt it, I shouldn't think he has the finesse for it. Still, perhaps we can change all that before you leave here.'

His softly spoken words conjured up erotic pictures in her mind, pictures of her and this man locked together in love. She blushed as she saw by the contempt in his eyes that he had clearly read her thoughts. 'You're disgusting!' she snapped to cover her embarrassment.

'Maybe,' he agreed huskily. 'But you seem to like me well enough.'

She didn't like him at all, her feelings went much deeper than that. How was it possible to fall in love with a man she hardly knew, a man still in love with the memory of a dead woman? No matter how it had happened she did love him, and it was because she loved him that she was going to stop fighting him about leaving here. If she stayed long enough she would be able to get out of marrying Nicholas simply by not turning up for the wedding—a coward's way out, but in this case the safest. Her father could be very persuasive when it came to getting something he wanted.

She couldn't have married Nicholas now, not even if Joel hadn't told her about his marriage to Nancy. How Joel Brent would laugh if he knew the mess she was in. How much more he would laugh if he knew she had fallen in love with him almost on sight.

'It's been tried before,' he told her coldly.

Sabina gave him a puzzled look. 'What has?'

'A colleague of yours, Sharon Kendal, got me into bed with her and then tried to get me to talk about Nicole. Needless to say I got the hell out of there.'

Sabina knew all about Sharon Kendal's methods of getting a story. She had come to work for the *Daily News* about six months ago, a hard-headed career woman of about Joel's age. In that six months she had come to be the chief reporter, pushing out anyone who got in her way. Sabina could quite well believe she would use any tactics to get a story, although how Joel could have fallen for that——

'I didn't know she was a reporter until it was too late.' Once again he seemed to be able to read her thoughts, a disconcerting habit of his.

She frowned. 'I thought you said you didn't tell her anything.'

His mouth quirked. 'I didn't mean too late for that.'

'Oh,' she blushed at her stupidity. 'Where are you going, Joel?' she changed the subject to something less painful to her. Joel Brent's past would be littered with women who had shared his bed—and Sabina found she hated every one of them.

'Downstairs—to sleep on the sofa. I'm not in the mood for you tonight, attractive as you are. Tell me, does Freed know exactly where in Scotland you are?'

He didn't even know she was in Scotland as far as she knew! 'Why should I tell you that?' she said defensively.

'He doesn't,' Joel said with satisfaction. 'This gets better and better.'

'How do you know he doesn't?' she flashed. 'I didn't say he——'

'He doesn't, Sabina. If he did you would have said so straight away.'

She sighed. 'You're right, he doesn't.'

'Now why should you admit that?' His eyes narrowed suspiciously. 'Is this another approach? Now that you know I won't be fooled by the holiday story are you going to try and charm it out of me?'

'I'm not interested in—in Nicole Dupont, or the relationship you had with her.'

'That's good,' Joel rasped. 'Because I don't intend discussing it with you. Get some sleep, Sabina, you look as if you need it.'

'Thanks!'

He laughed at her sarcasm. 'I'll leave Satan up here with you—just to keep you company,' he taunted.

'I'd rather you didn't,' she said hastily, the cat already watching her with an evil look in its eyes.

'I'm sure you would. Sweet dreams,' he mocked as he left.

Sweet dreams be damned! She couldn't even fall asleep, let alone dream. What was she going to do about Joel's bad opinion of her? Finding out that Nicholas was the man she was engaged to had only seemed to confirm that she was a reporter, and Joel made no secret of his hatred of reporters. With good reason, if she remembered correctly. Until he had been cleared of all suspicion of crashing deliberately, the newspapers had given him a rough time—mainly, she realised now, because he refused to confirm or deny their allegations.

If she could manage to convince Joel she wasn't a reporter perhaps he would stop resenting her and start seeing her as a woman. Telling him who her father was was definitely out, that would just damn her twice over in his eyes. Besides, if her father had known of Joel Brent's presence here he wouldn't be past using his daughter to get an exclusive interview. And if she knew that about her father then so did Joel.

She hated to think what was going to happen when her father found out she had changed her mind about marrying Nicholas. He would be furious.

A dark shadow loomed up and covered her, causing her to cry out. 'Be quiet, you little fool!' snapped the now familiar voice of Joel Brent.

'I—— You startled me!' she accused, sitting up to see that it was the flames from the fire that had made such a large shadow. Oh God, had he changed his mind about sleeping with her? She wasn't sure whether her heart leapt in fear or anticipation.

He placed a mug on the table beside her. 'That's no reason to scream the place down,' he told her impatiently. 'I've brought you some cocoa. You seem to be having trouble sleeping. The bed hasn't stopped creaking for the last fifteen minutes,' he explained how he had known of her sleeplessness.

'Sorry,' she mumbled, aware that she must have been keeping him awake too. She eyed the cocoa suspiciously.

Joel interpreted that look and smiled mockingly. 'It doesn't have anything in but a little sugar. I was never into drugs. Not my scene at all,' he taunted, his arms folded across his sweater-clad chest.

Sabina flushed. 'I don't talk like that, so there's no need to be sarcastic.'

'I'm so sorry, Miss Smith,' he said with exaggerated politeness. 'Put my rude behaviour down to lack of human company. All Satan requires of me is that I feed him, keep him warm, and occasionally give him a bit of love. Not so different from a woman, now I come to think of it.'

She sighed. 'I'm tired, Mr Brent. I'm not up to this verbal fencing right now.'

'Then drink your cocoa. Go on, it will help you sleep.'

'I haven't drunk cocoa since I was a child.' She sipped it tentatively, finding she still had a liking for it.

'And that was such a long time ago,' he teased softly, taking the empty mug out of her hand and pushing her down on to the pillow before zipping up her sleeping bag.

Sabina gave him a sleepy smile. 'Thank you—Daddy,' she did some teasing of her own, thankful that he had stopped sniping at her.

She had thought that too soon. 'Not me, Sabina,' he said harshly. 'Freed may be old enough to be that, but not me. And just to prove it . . .' His dark head swooped and his lips claimed hers.

Sabina's sleepiness instantly left her, her arms going up about his throat, her fingers entwining in the dark hair at his nape. She made no objection as he undid the buttons to her pyjama top, cupping her breast to gently arouse the nipple with his thumb. She instantly felt on fire, her whole body seeming to burn with a sensuality she had never before experienced.

Her neck arched, her head falling back as his mouth moved down to claim her, the first touch of a man's lips against her breast sending her into a world of wonder, a world where only Joel's caresses mattered, only his lips and hands on her body seemed important.

And then he was moving away from her, pulling her hands from about his neck. She looked at him with glazed passion-filled eyes. 'Joel . . .?' Her voice ached with her unfulfilment.

'I told you, I'm not in the mood for you tonight,' he said cruelly. 'You've been fed, there's the fire to keep you warm, and now you've had your loving.' He got up from the bed, looking down at her with flinty grey eyes. 'Now you should fall into as contented a sleep as Satan has.'

Her eyes darkened with pain, his rejection of her cutting into her like a knife. 'You're cruel!' she choked.

'And you're a very good actress. I could almost believe you enjoyed my caresses just now.'

'But I did!' she defended.

'Really? And what would you call that, job satisfaction?'

Sabina paled. 'If you think I responded to you just to try and get a story . . .'

'That's exactly what I think,' he told her coldly. 'I wonder if Freed knows how much you *enjoy* your work?'

'Get out of here!' She shook with anger, clutching the gaping front of her pyjama jacket to her. 'Get out and leave me alone!' To her shame tears welled up in her eyes.

Joel's eyes narrowed, his gaze moving slowly over each feature of her face. 'I think you may have chosen the wrong profession, Sabina. Your acting really is superb. Do you act when Freed makes love to you too? I should think you would have to, I can't see any woman willingly letting him touch her.' His mouth turned back in dislike.

The truth of the matter was that although Nicholas was attractive he had never aroused her, in fact the opposite, making her shut her mind off to him as he kissed and fondled her. Perhaps she had always subconsciously known he wasn't the man for her, a fact that had been proved when she responded mindlessly to Joel's caresses.

'I can see you do,' Joel scorned, his expression contemptuous. 'Is it worth it?'

She could see it wasn't now. But at the time she had wanted to please her father, had for once in her life wanted his full approval, and agreeing to marry Nicholas had certainly given her that.

'Don't bother to answer.' Joel moved to the door. 'And if you still can't sleep at least lie still. I have work to do tomorrow—today, and I need my sleep even if you don't.'

Her eyes widened. 'What work do you do?'

'Mind your own damned business!'

Once again she was alone, but infinitely sleepier than she had been a few minutes ago. But thoughts of Joel kept flooding into her mind. If he had to shut himself away from the world why on earth had he come to an out-of-the-way place like this, a cottage barely big enough for two people, a place where he had to do everything for himself? A man at the pinnacle of his profession, he had homes in every capital in Europe, a large apartment in New York, a yacht anchored off one of the Greek islands, and each of these homes was more than adequately staffed. And yet here he was, in a one-bedroomed cottage in Scotland.

He could also have had any amount of female company this last year, and yet he had chosen to remain here alone. But he wasn't alone now, she was here, and she would remain as long as he would let her. Which looked like being some time—she hoped.

Sabina woke once in the night, to feel something warm and soft pressing against her back, body warmth. Had Joel changed his mind and slept in the bed after all? She was almost afraid to turn and look, tensing as she slowly rolled over. Satan stirred beside her, sleepy green eyes suddenly becoming alert as he raised his head to look at her. Sabina moved her hand tentatively out of the sleeping bag, putting it down near the cat, as near as she dared. The black nose moved towards her, the mouth opening to show the viciously sharp teeth, before the rough tongue came out and licked her hand.

'Why, Satan,' she laughed softly, 'you old fraud!' She tickled him under the chin and he nuzzled his face into her hand, purring as loudly as he had for Joel. Finally the cat settled down again, even closer to her than he had been before. 'I hope I can make your master like me as easily,' she murmured before falling asleep again.

It was quite late in the morning when she woke, after nine, and she could hear a strange noise outside. Just as she was about to get up and investigate the noise stopped and she could hear someone, she supposed Joel, moving about downstairs. Satan had gone from the bedroom now, with nothing to show that they had become friends during the night.

'Are you going to lie there all day?' Joel rasped from the open doorway. 'I don't know what sort of life you lead in London,' he ducked his head to enter the room, his head only a couple of inches from the beamed ceiling as he straightened to his full height of well over six feet, 'but around here we get out of bed around seven o'clock.'

Sabina flushed at his rebuke, wishing she had had time to tidy herself before seeing him again. 'Has the mist cleared?' she asked.

'Yes. The sun's shining.'

'What was that noise I heard a few minutes ago?'

'From outside?'

'Mm,' she nodded.

'I was just chopping wood for the fire.' He pulled off his jumper. 'It will be cold tonight. I left it as late as I could before disturbing you,' he taunted, 'but I happen to want a shower and fresh clothes.'

That he had slept in his clothes was obvious, the cords were badly creased. 'You can't sleep downstairs tonight,' Sabina told him.

He eyed her tauntingly. 'I don't intend to. I'm going to sleep in that bed tonight.'

She looked at the vacant space next to her in the double bed. 'I—I see.'

'And you are going to sleep on the camp bed I found out in the shed,' he added mockingly.

Her eyes widened. 'A camp bed?'

'Mm,' he grinned. 'I think Mrs McFee must had had the occasional visitor.'

God, she thought, he looked so handsome when he smiled like that, more like the Joel Brent she re-

membered from his television spectaculars, the Joel
Brent who always looked and dressed impeccably.

His eyes darkened, all humour fading as he once again
seemed to be in her mind. 'But you can't be called a
welcome guest, can you? You've destroyed my peace,
forced me into looking for new accommodation. And
let me tell you, I don't appreciate your intrusion here.'

'I offered to leave.'

He gave a scornful laugh. 'Knowing damn well I
couldn't let you.' He pulled a dark green shirt out of a
chest of drawers. 'Get dressed and come downstairs. As
you're here you can do all the cooking.'

She struggled to sit up, her hair a tangled blond cloud.
'I'm not that good a cook!'

He shrugged. 'You can't be any worse than I am.
Besides, I like having a woman wait on me.'

Sabina glared at his back, sure that there had been
only too many women eager to do that. She got moodily
out of bed, searching through her saddle bags to find
some clean clothes. The weather seemed to have turned
warm again, as Joel had said, the mist had cleared and
it was a beautiful day, so Sabina chose to wear close-
fitting white cotton shorts and a pale green vest-top
tucked neatly into the narrow waistband of her shorts.
Her legs were long and shapely, and she wore rope sandals on her feet.

She met Joel's narrow-eyed look challengingly as he
came back from taking his shower, striving to remain
unmoved as his gaze lingered insolently on every youth-
ful curve of her body. 'Well?' she asked finally, the
silence unbearable.

The spell was broken, and he threw his discarded
clothes into a corner of the room, now wearing the dark
green shirt and black denims. 'You know you look
beautiful, desirable, you don't need me to confirm it.'

'Nevertheless,' she said huskily, 'I'd still like to hear it.'

He shook his head impatiently. 'Your approach certainly isn't subtle. But then I don't suppose you usually have the time for subtlety. Well, this time you have all the time in the world. Don't rush it, Sabina. The anticipation of eventually possessing that lovely body of yours will make the event all the sweeter.'

'Joel——'

'Not now, Sabina,' he kissed her abruptly on the mouth. 'Not until I'm more sure of your motives.'

'Satan seems sure of them.'

'He's a traitor of the first degree,' Joel dismissed, leading the way down the narrow stairs. 'I saw him snuggled up to you. In fact, I was quite jealous.'

Sabina coloured, remembering how she had wished that it had been Joel next to her. Thank goodness he had his back to her and so couldn't read her thoughts. He seemed to do that all too easily when he could actually see her face.

'Don't worry,' he obviously misunderstood her silence, 'I didn't sneak upstairs in the night to gaze at you as you slept.'

'I didn't think you had,' she snapped.

'I came to put more wood on the fire. Just making sure Satan kept warm,' he added dryly.

'Is he the only thing you care about? I'm sorry,' she bit her lip, 'I didn't mean to say that.'

His eyes narrowed. 'Why didn't you? It's the truth. I care for no one,' he told her harshly.

No one who was alive anyway! 'No, of course you don't. I—— Shall we have breakfast now, I think there's still some bacon and eggs left.'

Joel grasped her arm. 'What did you mean, Sabina? Why did you suddenly clam up like that?'

'It was nothing.' She gave a forced smile. 'Is bacon and eggs all right with you?'

'Don't lie to me.' He ignored her question about breakfast. 'We may only have known each other a matter of hours, but I can read you, Sabina. Your eyes tell me everything I want to know.' He gave a harsh laugh as she lowered her lashes. 'It's too late for that.'

'Where's the camp bed?' Sabina changed the subject, aware that he was becoming increasingly angry.

'That isn't important right now.'

'It is to me,' she insisted lightly. 'I want to make sure it's aired before I sleep on it.'

'It's outside in the sunshine. Satan's asleep on it, so I don't think it can be in too bad a condition. Now——'

'Cats always know the best places, don't they?' she chattered on nervously. 'I remember that as a child I——'

'Sabina!' his voice was icy. 'I'm sure that your childhood makes very interesting listening, but not at this moment.'

'I was only——'

His jaw was rigid. 'What's all this evasion about? Who do you think I care for?'

'No one,' she muttered.

'I can guess,' he scorned. 'I told you I won't be questioned about Nicole, or the relationship I had with her.' His expression was contemptuous. 'Don't try and trick answers out of me. If Sharon Kendal couldn't get a story out of me, for all of her dedication to duty, then a baby like you doesn't stand a chance.'

'I wasn't trying to trick you into doing anything,' she defended indignantly. 'I've already told you I'm not interested in the relationship between you and your mistress.'

He grasped her arm, his fingers digging painfully into

her flesh. 'Never call her my mistress again! Never, do you understand me?' he demanded furiously.

Her eyes were wide and frightened. 'I hear you, Joel.' She tried to prise his fingers loose, but they wouldn't be moved. 'I hear you!' she repeated tearfully.

He flung her away from him, not caring as she stumbled and almost fell. 'I never want to hear you mention her name again. Understood? Do you understand what I'm saying, Sabina?' he repeated harshly at her continued silence.

Yes, she understood, understood that his feelings for the Frenchwoman went so deep, were so special, that he wouldn't even allow anyone else to talk about her.

'Sabina?' he prompted, looming darkly over her.

'I—I understand,' she accepted dully, feeling as if her heart were breaking.

CHAPTER THREE

'WHERE are you going?'

Joel looked up, his hand on the door-handle of a room that led off to the left of the sitting-room. 'I'm not accustomed to answering to anyone for my movements,' he told her coldly.

'I—I was just wondering if I could put my camp bed up in there,' Sabina blushed.

'Well, you can't,' he snapped. 'I don't want you in this room at all.'

'But—but why?'

'There doesn't have to be a reason,' he said tautly. 'Just stay out of there. There's no lock on the door, and since you're a nosy little reporter your curiosity is probably working overtime, but if you ever go in this room your life won't be worth living.'

Sabina frowned. 'What do you have in there, for goodness' sake? A dead body?'

'Just stay out!' he rasped. 'What I have or have not in there is none of your concern.'

Oh God, she thought, he had that room set up as a sort of shrine to Nicole Dupont! How he must have loved her. And how ridiculous she was to feel jealous of a dead woman. But she couldn't fight someone who was dead! A living, breathing rival she could possibly cope with, a beautiful and treasured memory she couldn't even hope to beat.

'I'm sorry,' she turned away. 'I won't go in there, you have my word on it.'

'Your word!' Joel gave a taunting laugh. 'I have no

way of knowing if that means anything,' he derided.

'I've never broken my word,' she said indignantly. 'And I'll promise you something else—no one will ever find out your whereabouts from me.'

Grey eyes narrowed. 'You're using every trick in the book, aren't you?' he scorned. 'First there's the outrage, then there's the seduction routine, now it's the hand of friendship. Stick to the second one, Sabina, I'll enjoy it even if it gets you nowhere.'

'Are you going in there now?' she asked as he turned the door-handle in preparation of entering the room he had refused her admittance to. Not that she wanted to go in there anyway!

'Isn't that obvious?' he said dryly.

'Now?'

He nodded. 'I spend most of my days in here, nights too sometimes, and I don't see why I should change my routine for you. I have your word you won't leave the cottage, the word you say you never break?'

She flushed at his intended mockery. 'I'd like to go outside. For the sunshine!' she added at his suspicious look.

'Okay. But don't go wandering off. I'd find you before you got anywhere—and you would regret leaving here. I'd make sure of that.'

'I'm just going to keep Satan company,' she snapped resentfully.

'I'm sure he'll appreciate that,' Joel derided.

Her head went back defiantly. 'More than you would.'

His eyes mocked. 'Oh, I could appreciate you, Sabina—parts of you anyway.'

'Why are you so cynical?' she demanded angrily. She knew she was angering him and yet she wasn't prepared to take his insults any longer. 'I am not a reporter, I do not want to share your bed. And if you make one more comment like that to me I'll get away from here the first opportunity I get.' She held her breath as she waited for his reaction to her outburst.

Respect slowly entered those cynical grey eyes. 'Okay, Sabina, for the moment I'll cut the remarks—until I'm more sure of my facts,' the last was added threateningly. 'And I will be sure, as soon as it can be arranged.'

Her interest quickened. 'So you do have contact with someone?'

'Someone,' he nodded.

Sabina wondered if that 'someone' would be able to tell him that she was Charles Smith's daughter. She hoped not. But by the tone of Joel's voice he wasn't about to tell her the name of the person he kept in touch with.

'I'll be outside with Satan if you need me,' she told him absently.

'Need you?' he echoed harshly. 'Why the hell should I need *you*?'

'I just thought——'

'Well, don't! I don't *need* anyone!' He slammed into the other room.

That day seemed to set the pattern for the next three days. The camp bed had been set up in the bedroom and they had slept that way for the last three nights, Sabina on the camp bed and Joel in the bed, and not a word spoken between them once the light went off. They would breakfast together, on food that she had cooked for them, and then Joel would disappear into 'his room'.

They were almost like an old married couple, she thought humorously, talking casually in the evenings, on subjects that didn't inflame Joel's temper. Sabina had soon learnt which subjects to avoid, and she steered clear of them. The two of them had lapsed into a polite, if not quite friendly, camaraderie. Joel still didn't trust her, but he didn't suspect her every move any more.

And Satan spent each evening sitting on Sabina's lap, flexing and relaxing his claws into her leg in the ecstasy of his comfort. He wasn't as reserved as his master and unashamedly showed his appreciation of her company. He also lapped up every scrap of food she cared to give him.

On the fourth evening the routine was broken when Joel returned to 'his room' after dinner too. Sabina spent the evening glaring resentfully at the closed door, Satan's constant demands for attention seeming to point to him missing his master too.

Sabina bent to nuzzle into his black silky coat as once again he lay snuggled up on her denim-clad thighs. 'It isn't fair, Satan,' she mumbled crossly. 'We've been left on our own all day, and now that moody master of yours has left us alone again. I bet if I wasn't here he would allow you in there with him, wouldn't he? I bet——'

'His "moody master" doesn't allow Satan in there even when you aren't here,' interrupted an amused voice.

'Joel!' she blushed guiltily.

'Yes—Joel,' he smiled completely, the first time he had ever done so in her presence. 'And Satan is never allowed in there with me because he breaks my concentration.'

Sabina was fascinated by his smile, her heart beating faster at the charm in his relaxed features. 'Concentration on what?' she asked vaguely. 'And why are you looking so pleased with yourself?'

'Because I've finished.' He gently pushed Satan on to

the floor. 'Time to make room for the big boys.' He took Satan's place, lying full length on the sofa, his head resting on Sabina's lap. 'God, this sofa is uncomfortable! But you aren't.' He settled into the curve of her thighs, looking up at her with warm grey eyes. 'Miss me?' His voice was huskily seductive.

'You know I have,' once again she blushed. 'It's no fun sitting here on my own.'

He took hold of her hand, draping her arm across his chest as he played with her fingers. 'There hasn't been any fun for you at all since you came here. Would you like to change that?'

Sabina stiffened, trying to pull her hand away, but Joel refused to let go; if anything his grip tightened. 'What do you mean?' she asked finally.

Joel laughed at her wary expression, sitting up and turning to face her. 'Not what you obviously think I mean,' he taunted. 'Use your common sense, Sabina. I've had the chance the last few nights to make love to you if I had felt so inclined, but——'

'Have you now?' her eyes sparkled angrily. 'I might have had something to say about that!'

'I'm sure you would,' he smiled.

His amusement angered Sabina even more. 'I would have said no,' she told him adamantly.

'I'm sure,' he nodded, giving the opposite impression to his words. 'Now, what I was suggesting a few minutes ago was that we go out.'

Her eyes widened. She had been a prisoner of this cottage for four days now—and she wasn't sure she wanted to be free ever again. She liked being with Joel. 'The two of us, go out?' she asked incredulously.

'Well, I don't see anyone else in the room, so I would presume I meant you and me.'

'Will you stop mocking me!'

Joel sighed. 'I'm not mocking, Sabina. I asked if you want to go out, yes or no?'

'Yes. But——'

He stood up. 'Then let's go.' He looked at his wrist-watch, his shirt sleeves turned back almost to his elbows. 'We don't have a lot of time left to get there.'

She scrambled to her feet. 'To get where?'

'The hotel you stayed in the other night. I thought we might go and have a drink.'

'That would be nice. But—but won't you be—recognised?'

'Only as Joe Bradley. That's what they know me as around here.'

She pulled on her coat, as usual the evening having turned cold. 'You mean no one has recognised you here?' she asked disbelievingly.

'No one. Maybe they've all led sheltered lives,' he mocked.

'Incredible!' She shook her head.

'Not really. You didn't recognise me to start with. I don't exactly look the part, now do I?'

'But even so . . .'

'I like it this way. I've had too many years when everything I did seemed to make the headlines. The press just never let up.' Harshness had entered his voice. 'Let's go,' he said curtly, 'before I change my mind.'

Sabina frowned. 'Will we make it in time, it's getting late?'

'I have a car.'

'A—a car?' she gasped. 'But I've never seen it!'

'It's in a garage down the track, in the opposite direction to the way you arrived. I very rarely use it, I usually borrow a horse to go riding from one of the farms. Wait until you see the car,' he chuckled. 'I bought it from one of the locals. Before the four accidents its previous

owner had in it I think it was a well-preserved Austin
A40. The owner was banned from driving for three years
after the last accident, hence its sale.'

It was indeed a battered wreck of a car, a sort of
rusty pale blue colour, with a black obviously hand-
painted roof. The seats had seen better days too, ripped
in parts, with some of the stuffing sticking out of the
leather.

'Good grief!' Sabina couldn't help her gasp of dismay.
'It's awful!'

'I know,' Joel chuckled, opening the passenger door
for her. 'But my Porsche would have been a bit conspicuous around here. Your carriage awaits, milady,' he
mocked.

She got in. 'I think some of the springs have gone in
my seat,' she winced as the car made the bumpy journey
down the track on to the road.

'I shouldn't be at all surprised,' he acknowledged
lightly.

'Will Satan be all right on his own?' They had left the
cat curled up in front of the log fire, wearily opening
one eye to watch their noisy departure.

'I should think so,' he derided. 'Although since you
arrived and keep feeding him tasty little morsels, from
your own plate most of the time, he hasn't been out
mousing as often as he used to.'

Sabina's nose wrinkled with distaste. 'He went out
this afternoon and caught one. He brought it back and
put it at my feet.' She swallowed hard. 'It was dead.'

Joel nodded. 'Cats are tormenting creatures. Satan
probably played with it until it died of fright. I hope
you thanked him for his gift.'

She grimaced. 'I most certainly did not! I threw him
out of the cottage, the mouse quickly followed him.'

'Poor Satan. He was only being friendly.'

'Then he can be friendly with someone else. It made me feel sick.'

'It's only nature. And I'm all for nature.' His voice deepened meaningly.

Sabina felt the warm colour enter her cheeks. 'You haven't told me what we're celebrating,' she chose to change the subject, too conscious of her own awareness of this man. 'What did you just finish?'

'The work I came here to do.'

'But what——'

'If you start asking questions again, Sabina, I'll take you straight back to the cottage,' he warned her firmly. 'Now do we go on or turn back?' He slowed the car down almost to a standstill.

'On,' she answered in a stilted voice.

His hand came out to touch her cheek. 'You bring my anger down on you. Why can't you just forget your reason for being here? I'm trying hard to do just that,' he added grimly.

'I'd rather not. You see, whether you believe this or not, I came to Scotland to make my mind up about marrying Nicholas. I'm sure now that he isn't the right person for me.'

'And how did you make this startling discovery?' Joel derided.

'I realised I was in love with someone else.' She looked at him with unflinching eyes, her emotions openly displayed for him to read if he cared to.

'Who—' he broke off, shaking his head as he looked at her. 'Oh no, Sabina. I may be all kinds of a fool, made mistakes about people in the past, but I'm not stupid enough to fall for that old trick. Although you do it better than most, I must admit,' he added tautly.

Sabina frowned, aware that this had gone far from

the way she had wanted it to. But what had she expected, a declaration of love from him in return? That she had fallen in love with him in a matter of hours was unusual enough, to expect him to feel the same way would be asking for a miracle. But she wasn't ashamed of telling him how she felt about him, although his reaction was rather puzzling.

'Do what better than most?' she asked him.

'Your job, Sabina. You do your job very well. What's the matter? Is your time for getting this story nearly up and you're getting desperate?' he scorned.

'I don't understand you. You——'

'But I understand you,' he turned the car into the hotel forecourt. 'I understand you very well. But pretending to be in love with me won't get you your story either. I'm sorry, Sabina, but your fiancé is out of luck this time. I am not going to talk to you.'

Her eyes flashed her anger. 'You cynical bastard!' Her hand moved and struck him forcibly on the cheek. 'I hate you!' She would have pummelled him with her fists, but he caught hold of her around the wrists, exerting painful pressure to the delicate bones there.

'No one hits me.' His face was a livid mask of anger. 'And especially not a woman. You need taming, little vixen, and if Nicholas Freed isn't man enough to do it, I will!' He pulled her against the hardness of his body, grinding his mouth down on hers.

Sabina fought for all she was worth, but it was a battle she had lost almost before it began, her treacherous body arching against him, her lips against his pleading for his gentleness. But there was no gentleness in him, only hard demand and contempt.

It was the contempt that finally made her stop kissing him back, causing her to freeze in his embrace. The message finally seemed to get through to him and he thrust her away from him, wiping his mouth with the back of his hand.

Sabina pushed open her car door, getting out on to the tarmaced car park to take huge gulps of air into her lungs. She glared at Joel as he got out the other side. 'I'm not tamed, Mr Brent,' she told him vehemently. 'And I never will be.'

'We'll see about that.' His eyes were narrowed to steely slits as he bent to lock the car doors.

The thought of spending time in the hotel trying to appear as if everything were all right between them now seemed impossible. 'I'd rather go back to the cottage,' she said abruptly.

Joel took hold of her arm and pushed her in the direction of the entrance to the bar. 'I want a drink,' he snapped. 'So you can damn well come with me.'

Sabina went and sat on one of the bench seats in the corner of the room, noting that there were only half a dozen or so other people in the room, a couple of men sitting in the opposite corner, and a party of four who looked like holidaymakers in their bright casual clothing, their mood boisterous.

She couldn't even look at Joel as he placed the glass of Martini and lemonade on the table in front of her, pretending an interest in the two young men talking at the table opposite, an interest she was far from feeling.

'I think he likes you too,' Joel drawled beside her.

Sabina turned, almost recoiling as she realised just how close he was sitting, his sensual mouth only inches away. By turning she had also brought their thighs close together on the bench-seat, Joel's arm resting along the back of her part of the seat.

She blinked nervously. 'I'm sorry . . .?' She showed her puzzlement.

His expression was cold. 'The man you keep staring at, he returns you interest.'

'What man——? Oh,' she blushed as she realised he must have seen her watching the two men and misconstrued that look. 'I wasn't staring at him,' she snapped. 'I wasn't staring at anyone, just showing a natural curiosity about our fellow drinkers.'

'Strange that both he and I got the same impression.' Joel sipped what looked like neat whisky. 'He can't take his eyes off you.'

'Really?' She gave the man another quick glance. Yes, he was staring at her, and now his friend was turning to look at her too. She was beginning to feel uncomfortable, half turning her back on them as she tried to ignore them. 'Perhaps I remind them of someone,' or perhaps they remembered her photograph in the newspapers when she became engaged to Nicholas! This seemed the more likely explanation. 'Or perhaps you do,' she added mockingly.

Joel gave her a scathing glance, his impatience barely controlled. 'They aren't looking at me.'

'And does that rankle?' she taunted.

'What did you say?' he rapped out, his mouth a thin ominous line.

Sabina instantly regretted her bitchiness. She had never found him in the least conceited. 'I'm sorry. I——'

'You damn well will be,' he threatened in a soft dangerous voice. 'When I get you home.'

'Home?' she echoed, her eyebrows high.

'The cottage,' he corrected tersely. He stood up. 'Let's go.'

'But I haven't even touched my drink!'

'Too bad, I've finished mine, and as I have the transport you leave with me.'

'But——'

'I still have your belongings, Sabina, if you were thinking of making a run for it. I'm sure our young friend over there would be only too glad to look after you for a couple of days—for a price. A price you seem only too willing to pay,' he added sneeringly. 'Not again!' he clamped her arm to her side as she would have struck him for the second time this evening. 'God, that temper of yours needs controlling!'

'You were insulting me again,' there were tears in her eyes now. 'Just because I let you kiss me it doesn't mean I would let that man too.'

'Girls like you aren't too discriminatory,' he said abruptly. 'Come on,' he dragged her towards the door, 'let's get out of here.'

Sabina resisted. 'There's no need to be so—so *savage!*' she told him angrily. 'People are staring,' she hissed.

'I couldn't give a damn.' He pushed her outside. 'They'll probably put my behaviour down to a natural desire to be alone with you.'

'There's nothing *natural* about you,' she informed him as she got angrily into the car. 'You're completely *un*-natural!'

He glared at her in the dark confines of the car. 'Would you rather have stayed and chatted up your young admirer? He had just got up the courage to speak to you and was coming over to our table,' he told her grimly.

'I don't believe you. He could see I was with you. Why should——'

'Look behind you,' Joel ordered as they left the hotel car park. 'Go on, look.'

Sabina did so, her eyes widening as she saw the blond one of the two men standing just outside the hotel staring after them, his frustration with their departure obvious. 'I still think he must have recognised you,' she told Joel defensively.

'Maybe. God, you've done nothing but cause me trouble since you appeared out of the mist. I should have thrown you out that first evening.'

'You wouldn't let me go.'

'I should have thrown you out, reporter or no reporter.' He gave her an impatient look. 'I should have ignored the desirability of long golden hair and huge green eyes.' His own eyes darkened in colour. 'I've just made it more difficult for myself,' he muttered.

'Made what difficult?'

'Not telling you everything, not taking you to my bed and confessing my very soul to you. God,' he groaned, 'how tempted I am!'

'Joel——'

'No!' his hands gripped the steering-wheel. 'Don't try any of your tricks on me now. If I took you I would lose what little self-respect I have left. And while I may enjoy it at the time I would only make you suffer for it afterwards.'

'Joel, please——'

'No more declarations of love, Sabina,' he scorned. 'That's just asking too much. I'll be leaving here soon, very soon in fact, and——'

'Where are you going?' Her eyes were wide in her panic. He couldn't just disappear again, go out of her life for ever. If hundreds of reporters hadn't managed to find him this time then she felt sure she wouldn't stand a chance of finding him if he chose to go off again.

He gave a mocking, humourless smile. 'Wouldn't you like to know? I have some advice for you, Sabina. Get out of this business, get out before it destroys you. It isn't too late, there's still a sweet little girl inside you trying to get out. Forget about being a reporter, forget about marrying Freed. Find yourself a nice boy to marry, and have half a dozen kids. *That's* what you should be, a wife and mother, not some hardbitten reporter who'll do anything for a story.'

'Joel, I——'

'Do you want to be Freed's next punch-bag?' he demanded savagely. 'Do you?'

'No. But——'

'Then forget him. Give him back his rock and get the hell out of there.'

Sabina frowned at his vehemence. 'Why are you so concerned about what I do with my life?' she probed. 'You don't even like me.'

'I like you, too much to see you making such a big mistake.'

'You—you like me?'

'I like what you could be,' he corrected tersely, parking the car.

Sabina walked down the rough track beside him, the darkness enclosing them in an intimacy Joel seemed anxious to put behind them, striding ahead with no thought for her much shorter legs.

She put a hand on his arm, feeling him tense beneath her touch. 'What could I be, Joel?' she asked huskily.

'I already told you that.' He shook off her hand, throwing his jacket off as soon as they entered the cottage, heading straight for the room he had told her not to enter.

'Are you going to work—now?' Her disappointment was obvious.

His grey gaze was rapier-sharp. 'I've heard it's a good substitute,' he taunted, shutting the door firmly in her face.

Well, if he thought he had got rid of her for the night he was mistaken! She would stay down here on the sofa until he decided to come out. She wouldn't just be pushed out of his life. She wouldn't!

It was very dark when she woke up, the fire almost out, and Satan seated on her lap for what warmth he could find. And there was still a light on under the door to the other room, which meant Joel was still working. Whatever that was! What work could he be doing in there for hours on end in complete silence? Sabina couldn't even begin to guess.

She gave a groan as she stood up, every bone in her body seeming to ache. 'I was right about that sofa, boy,' she spoke in a whisper to the cat. 'It's more than just uncomfortable, it's more like a form of torture.' She rubbed a particularly sore spot at the base of her spine.

The room was suddenly flooded with light as the door behind her opened and Joel stared at her in disbelief. 'You haven't been to bed,' he said in amazement.

Sabina grimaced. 'How clever of you to guess.'

His eyes narrowed. 'Why haven't you?'

'I was waiting for you,' her head went back challengingly.

He strode forward, swinging her up into his arms as she seemed to sway. 'Don't you ever give up?' he rasped.

Her arms were up about his throat, and she rested her head wearily on his shoulder. 'I didn't want you to leave without me.'

Joel walked up the stairs with her, throwing her down on the bed, standing over her looking like the devil himself. 'When I decide to leave here I'll let you know.'

'Promise?' Her eyelids drooped tiredly.

He sighed. 'I promise. Just get to sleep, Sabina,' he said wearily. He shook his head. 'We have to talk. Tomorrow, hmm?' He sounded almost gentle.

She nodded eagerly. 'Oh yes, Joel.'

'And I don't mean about the past,' he rasped. 'I want

to talk about you and me, not Nicole.'

'Yes, Joel.' She gave him a sweet smile, her hair splayed out across the pillow.

His features relaxed slightly as he continued to look down at her. 'Here,' he picked Satan up and put him on the bed beside her. 'Your willing slave,' he mocked. 'You might as well stay in my bed. I won't be sleeping tonight, and there isn't room for you and Satan on the camp bed.'

'Thank you.' She snuggled down into the pillow that smelt sensuously of Joel and the aftershave he always wore.

'That cat adores you,' he chuckled as Satan made himself comfortable under her chin. 'I think you'll have to take him with you when you go, he'll be lost without you now.'

'Do I have to go? Couldn't I stay here, with you?'

'I told you,' he said harshly. 'I'll be leaving soon.'

'Couldn't I come with you?' she pleaded.

'I've said we'll talk tomorrow.' He moved to the door. 'Things always seem clearer in the light of day.' He threw a log on the fire before quietly leaving the room.

Sabina was in a mood of quiet anticipation as she washed and dressed the next day, carrying Satan downstairs with her when she was ready. Joel was in the lounge, just pulling on his jacket.

'You—you're going out?' she asked nervously.

He picked up a long inch-thick parcel. 'I'm just going to post this. I won't be long.'

She put Satan down. 'I'll come with you.'

'I'll only be gone about ten minutes, Sabina,' he said impatiently. 'You stay here and cook breakfast.'

'You—you'll come back?'

'I don't like clinging women, Sabina,' he told her harshly. 'I never have. I'll be back—in my own time,' he snapped as she was about to ask him when.

Her bottom lip trembled at his hard attitude. 'I'm sorry,' she mumbled.

He seemed to hesitate at the door, finally relenting and coming over to where she stood looking so forlorn. 'No, I'm the one that's sorry,' he said softly, smoothing away her tears with his thumb tips. 'You're either the most sensitive female I know or you're still continuing that act. Which is it, Sabina?'

Her answer was to launch herself into his arms, her face buried in his chest. 'It isn't an act, Joel,' her voice was muffled. 'Really it isn't.'

'Okay,' he held her at arm's length. 'I'll be back in a few minutes,' he bent to kiss her lightly on the nose. 'And I'd like my food waiting on the table for me when I get here.'

Sabina smiled through her tears. 'You Tarzan, me Jane,' she teased.

'That's right, woman,' he returned her smile before he left.

Sabina happily set about getting their breakfast, humming softly to herself as she moved about the cramped kitchen. It was going to be all right between them, she was sure of it.

When she heard a noise out in the lounge a few minutes later she rushed out to greet Joel, stopping short as she saw the two men from the hotel the evening before now standing in the middle of Joel's lounge. And as Joel wasn't back yet they had entered the cottage without being invited to!

'What are you doing here?' she demanded indignantly.

The younger one, the one who had been staring at her in the hotel, was the one to answer her. 'Where's Brent gone?' he asked curtly.

Sabina couldn't hide her start of surprise. 'I'm sorry,' she shook her head in pretended puzzlement, 'I don't know who you mean.'

The dark-haired one, a man of about thirty, smiled at her reaction. 'We mean Joel Brent, love,' he smirked, his stance challenging.

'Joel Brent?' she feigned surprise. 'Oh, you must mean my husband.' She couldn't stop the hot colour that entered her cheeks at the thought of really being married to Joel. Just the thought of it made her feel dizzy. 'He's often taken for Joel Brent,' she added for good measure.

'We aren't falling for that one,' the blond man derided. 'We know exactly who he is. Just as we know who you are—Miss Smith.'

Sabina went white. 'I think there's been some sort of mistake. My name is Bradley. I live here with my husband.'

The dark-haired man shook his head, took out his wallet and produced a photograph. He held it out towards her. Sabina took it with a shaking hand. It was a photograph of herself, not the usual ones the newspapers printed from time to time, but one taken of her on the holiday she had had in Monte Carlo with her father earlier in the year.

She looked dazedly at the two men. 'But this——'

'Was taken by your father,' the blond one finished. 'And that's who we got it from.'

Sabina swallowed hard. 'You mean——'

'I mean we work for your father, Miss Smith,' he supplied in a bored voice. 'And we're here to take you back to London.'

CHAPTER FOUR

SABINA bit her lip, turning away. Her father had sent these men! She should have guessed, should have known he wouldn't let her take this holiday. He had controlled her life ever since she could remember, sent her to all the right schools, allowed her to be friends only with the girls he considered to be in the same social bracket as themselves, their families respectable, their wealth matching their own. He had even chosen her husband for her, she saw that now, and not once during her nineteen years had he let her out of his sight for more than a day or so. Her bid for independence at this late stage must have come as something of a shock to him.

'How did you find me?' she asked huskily; that photograph had been too obviously her for her to keep up the pretence any longer.

'We can talk about that on the drive back to London,' the dark-haired one dismissed. 'When are you expecting Brent back?'

Joel! Oh God, Joel! She didn't want to leave him, go away from here and possibly never see him again. 'He should be back any moment,' she told them absently. 'But I——'

'Then we'd better get moving,' the blond one interrupted. 'You take Miss Smith out to the car, Ray, and I'll tidy things up here.'

The one called Ray took hold of her arm and pulled her towards the cottage door. Sabina gave him her most haughty look, feeling his fingers loosen, but he maintained a hold on her. 'I'm not leaving here until I've seen Mr Brent,' she told them coldly, every inch Charles Smith's daughter in that moment.

'Mike?' the dark-haired man she knew as Ray appealed to his companion, obviously the stronger of the two.

Mike sighed. 'Your father's instructions were to get you out of here immediately. And I for one am not willing to argue with him,' he told her dryly.

Few people were, that was the trouble. The only person who ever disagreed with him was Nicholas—and she was supposed to be having him as her husband. God, she thought, it would like exchanging one gaoler for another! Thank heaven she had changed her mind about that marriage.

'I am,' she said firmly. 'I'm not leaving until I've spoken to Jo—Mr Brent.'

Mike raised his eyebrows resignedly. 'Ray,' he cocked his head towards the door.

Ray gasped. 'You mean——'

'I mean carry her out,' his friend confirmed. 'You know what Mr Smith's instructions were, if she won't leave voluntarily then we're to use force.'

'Okay,' Ray shrugged. 'I'm sorry about this, Miss Smith,' his arms went about her waist and he lifted her into the air, 'but I don't have any choice.'

'Yes, you do!' She struggled in his arms. 'Put me down! *Put me down*, I tell you!'

'Mike . . .'

'Get her out of here,' his friend ordered. 'I'll get her things together and join you in a minute,' and he moved towards the closed door.

'Not in there!' Sabina cried, struggling more ferociously. Ray was stronger than he looked because she wasn't able to break out of his grasp. 'You can't go in there!' she told Mike angrily, glaring at him.

His answer was to open the door. Satan slipped in between his feet as he entered the room. 'Well, well,' they heard him murmur, 'so that's what he's been up to. Hey, Ray, come and look at this.'

'What is it?' Ray carried Sabina to the doorway.

What she saw there made her gasp. This was no shrine to Nicole Dupont as she had imagined it to be. It was a music room. A huge piano stood in the middle of the room, hundreds of screwed-up music sheets on the floor. Joel had been writing music all the time he had been in here!

But she had never heard a piano playing—and Joel said he had been working the last few days. What lengths he had gone to just to prevent her knowing what he was doing! He must have been working on his music without the use of a piano, just so that she wouldn't know he was composing.

'Wow!' Ray breathed softly. 'So this is why he suddenly dropped out of sight.'

All the fight had gone out of Sabina. *What* had Joel been composing? Could it possibly have something to do with the parcel he had just gone off to post?

Mike suddenly sprang into action, glancing hurriedly at his wrist-watch. 'Okay, let's move. We don't want to come up against Brent.' His gaze raked insolently over Sabina. 'He may not like us stealing away his—little companion.'

Sabina flushed at his implication. 'I'm sure that when my father employed you he didn't intend you to insult me.' Her tone was haughty.

'Maybe not,' he acknowledged grudgingly. 'Get going, Ray. And take—Miss Smith with you.'

Once again she was hauled into Ray's arms. 'But my—my bicycle!' she stupidly protested about the first thing that came into her head, hoping to delay them long enough for Joel to return. 'I mean, it isn't mine. I have to——'

'It's already been taken care of.'

'H-How?'

'Simple,' Mike shrugged. 'We bought it.'

Of course. Her father bought out whole companies, why shouldn't he buy a simple bicycle? 'But I——'

'No more arguments, Miss Smith,' he told her. 'Your father wants you back, and we aim to see he gets you. You've shocked him, you know. He had no idea you even knew Brent, let alone that you were shacking up with him. Now he wants you home before there's any scandal.'

Her eyes widened, her face pale. 'Sc-scandal? What sort of scandal?'

'With you removed from here it shouldn't be a scandal, just a sensation. With you off the scene your father can publicise the whereabouts of the elusive Joel Brent, even what he's been doing this last year. But it wouldn't be possible if you were known to have been living with Brent this last week.'

Sabina was very pale. 'But you know!'

Mike smiled. 'And we've been paid very handsomely to keep our mouths shut.' He flicked a glance at his friend. 'I'll be two minutes collecting the stuff that we need.'

Ray managed to get Sabina into the car they had parked down the dirt driveway, the fight mainly gone out of her. She had ruined everything for Joel. If her father hadn't sent these men up here to look for her they would never have found Joel. How he was going to hate her for this! And she couldn't blame him.

When Mike came out of the cottage he threw some things into the boot of the car before getting in behind the wheel. 'Just the one bedroom, Miss Smith,' he taunted. 'And just the one bed too.' He put the car into gear and they slowly moved off down the bumpy track.

Sabina turned to look out of the back window. The cottage had been home to her the last few days. Satan sat outside in the sunshine washing his black glossy coat, unaware that she was going away from him and his master for good.

As the cottage disappeared from view she turned dejectedly in her seat. The man Mike was right about there only being one bed in evidence, the camp bed was packed away each morning, the bedroom too small to accommodate both beds if you wanted to move about the room. It was obvious what conclusion this hateful man had come to.

'Keep your dirty thoughts to yourself,' she snapped. 'I don't appreciate them and I don't think my father would either.'

'From the way your father reacted on the telephone last night I think you could hear more of the same from him,' Mike smiled. 'Just calm yourself, Miss Smith. This is going to be a long trip, with no stops, on your father's orders, and I don't think you bitching at us all the way is going to make it any more enjoyable.'

He was right, it was a long trip, and it wasn't enjoyable. Despite the power and speed of the Mercedes it still took ten hours to complete the drive back to London, ten hours when the only stops had been for petrol and the snack food they had eaten going along.

Sabina hadn't been able to eat a thing, her thoughts all with Joel. When he came back and found her gone, his music-room invaded, he was going to think he had been right about her all along.

And from what Mike had said her father intended doing a story on Joel. Joel would think it was her doing, would hate and despise her, and just at a time when he had seemed to be starting to trust her, to like her even.

The apartment she shared with her father was ablaze with lights when they finally arrived back in London that evening. She was obviously expected.

She got out of the car. 'Thank you,' she said with cold politeness. 'I can find my own way now.'

'No way,' Mike smilingly shook his head. 'You aren't going to give us the slip now. Your father told us to deliver you to him personally, and that's exactly what we're going to do.'

Her head went back haughtily, her contempt for these two men a tangible thing. 'As you wish.' She led the way, greeting Simon, the butler, before going through to the lounge.

Her father was alone in the room, and instantly stood to his feet when he saw her enter the room. 'Sabina!' his relief was evident as he gathered her into his arms. 'Thank God you're back!'

Sabina held herself aloof, moving gracefully out of his embrace. 'You knew I was returning, your blood-hounds made sure of that.'

'Okay, boys,' her father dismissed them. 'I'll see you tomorrow.'

'For the pay-off,' Sabina scorned bitterly.

Her father sighed. 'Tomorrow,' he repeated, watching as the two men left. 'Now why the hell did you have to get nasty with them? They were only carrying out my instructions.'

Her eyes flashed like emeralds. 'I'm well aware of that,' she snapped. 'What I want to know is why. I go away for a holiday and you send men out looking for——'

'A holiday!' her father cut in angrily, his still hand-some face flushed. At fifty, he was still capable of turn-ing many a female head, his iron-grey hair brushed back from his forehead, his tanned face unlined with age, his tall body lithe and muscular. He had his women, Sabina knew that, but he always claimed no one could ever take the place of her mother in his life.

'Yes, a holiday,' she answered with equal anger. 'I wanted a couple of weeks of freedom, a couple of weeks to think, to——'

'To move in with Joel Brent,' he finished furiously. 'Do you have any idea what Nicholas would do if he knew about that?'

Her eyebrows rose. 'You mean he doesn't already?'

'Of course not.' He began pacing up and down the room. 'If he did he would call off the wedding.'

'Good.' Sabina sat down. 'That's exactly what I want him to do.'

That stopped her father's pacing, and he came to stand in front of her. 'What did you say?' he asked softly, disbelievingly.

She looked at him with steady green eyes. 'I don't want to marry Nicholas.'

His mouth set in an ominous line. 'On the basis of a few days spent in Scotland with Brent you've decided to call off your engagement? Good God, girl, the wedding is only seven weeks away!'

'*Was* in seven weeks' time. As soon as I see Nicholas I intend telling him I've changed my mind.'

Her father drew a ragged breath. 'I wish you wouldn't do that.'

'I don't love him, Dad!' It was a cry for understanding. 'Did you know that he actually hit his last wife?'

'I suppose Brent told you that?' he scorned.

'Is it true?'

'Rumours, Sabina,' he dismissed. 'Just rumours.'

'Were they? I don't think so, Joel said——'

'Yes—Joel!' again he interrupted her. 'How the hell

long have you known him?'

'What does that matter? You haven't answered my questions about Nicholas.'

'Okay, okay!' he snapped. 'So he and Nancy used to argue a lot, and maybe he did hit her once or twice, I can't remember. But you're nothing like Nancy——'

'And I suppose that makes it all right?' Sabina demanded to know. 'How long do you think I'll be able to defend myself against the powerful man Nicholas undoubtedly is?'

'It wasn't like that between them. They argued, mainly because Nancy used to goad him into it. But you aren't like her, you're much more mature than she was.'

'How nice!'

'Sabina——'

'Don't tell me it's wedding nerves!' She stood up forcefully, her fragility belied by the fierceness of her expression. 'I'm not nervous about marrying Nicholas—because there isn't going to be a wedding.'

'You have to marry him, Sabina,' her father told her quietly.

Her eyes widened. 'What do you mean?'

'Exactly what I said.'

'I *have* to marry him?' she repeated dazedly.

'Yes,' he sighed. 'Unless you want to see me ruined.'

'Don't be silly, Dad,' she scoffed. 'We can weather a little scandal like a broken engagement. I realise things could be a bit awkward with Nicholas for a while, but that will pass. In time it will be——'

'Nicholas has the power to ruin me, Sabina,' he informed her softly, unable to meet her eyes.

She breathed deeply, suddenly still. 'How?'

'A few months ago I invested in some bad deals. I—I borrowed money from Chasnick Enterprises to bail myself out.'

Chasnick, a name derived from the two men's first names, Charles and Nicholas, was the company formed for the running of their newspaper and magazines. Sabina knew that both men had their own personal business interests, but it had always been agreed between them that Chasnick Enterprises would never enter into those dealings. It seemed her father had broken the rules.

'And Nicholas found out,' she said dully, feeling as if a cage door were shutting behind her.

'Not yet,' he sighed. 'But he will at the end of the year, when the accounts are made up.'

'I see,' she voiced slowly. 'And you wanted me to marry him so that you had leverage to stop his prosecuting you?'

'I don't think he would go that far, but the scandal of my deceiving my partner isn't going to do me much good.' He bit his lip. 'But you always seemed fond of him, Sabina, I would never have encouraged things between you otherwise.'

'Wouldn't you?' she said bitterly.

He flushed. 'No, of course I wouldn't. No one forced you into this marriage, Sabina. It seemed to be what you wanted.'

'You didn't encourage it, Dad, but then you didn't discourage it either. All that talk about what a fine man he is, how he would always take care of me. I wonder if someone told Nancy Freed that rubbish too,' she said scornfully. 'And look how true it was for her!'

'You have no idea how it turned out for her. They just weren't suited, that's all.'

'That's your opinion. God, how can you see me married to a monster like that?' she cried.

'Has he ever shown any signs of being violent with you?'

'No. But——'

'Then trust your own judgment, not what other people tell you. Nicholas has always been very gentle with you. You have to marry him, Sabina. Nicholas wants you, and he has the means to force the issue. Unless you want to see me ruined?'

'No, you know I don't. But——'

'Then marry him. Heaven knows I wish it could be different, but I can't see any other way out of it. This time spent with Brent can't have been anything serious, and——'

Sabina's eyes flashed. 'How can you be sure of that?'

'Because it's obvious. You hardly know the man.'

'I know him well enough, well enough to love him! We've been alone together for almost a week, Dad. Doesn't that tell you anything?'

He seemed to go pale. 'You mean——'

'That we were lovers?' she finished calmly. 'And if we were? Do you think Nicholas will be able to accept that?'

Her father looked scathing. 'I don't believe you, Sabina. You've been staying with Joel Brent, but I don't believe there was any more to it than that.'

She shrugged. 'Ask your two little spies. They could tell you there was only the one bedroom at the cottage.'

'So you slept downstairs,' her father dismissed. 'Or he did. It doesn't matter which.'

'We both slept in the bedroom,' Sabina told him quietly.

'No!' he gasped.

'Yes. How do you think Nicholas will like knowing I've been on holiday in the wilds of Scotland with Joel Brent?'

Her father almost seemed to flinch. 'Well, as he believes you to have been staying with your Aunt

Daphne, suffering from an attack of pre-wedding nerves, he might find any talk of Scotland a little hard to take.'

'Nicholas believes—he thinks I've been in Bedfordshire?'

'Well, I had to tell him something when you just disappeared like that.'

'Wouldn't the truth have been more advisable?' she taunted.

'Not on your life! It's bad enough that I've been scouring the countryside for you, if Nicholas had known you had just disappeared into the blue there would have been hell to pay. He only agreed not to call Daphne's house because I told him I thought you would be better for being left alone.'

Sabina sighed. 'And when is he expecting me back from this little visit to Aunt Daphne's?'

Her father flushed at her scathing tone. 'As soon as Mike and Ray called to say they'd found you I let Nicholas know you were coming home. He'll be round first thing tomorrow.'

'And am I supposed to act the contrite fiancée?' she demanded angrily. 'Beg his forgiveness for being a silly little girl?'

'Well . . .'

'I won't do it! I can't marry him,' she said desperately. 'I—I love Joel.'

'You hardly know the man!' her father exploded. 'You can't do, I've never heard you mention him.'

'I would hardly tell my own father about my secret lover.'

'You have to marry Nicholas. If you don't I'll—I'll——'

'Yes?' Sabina challenged. 'You'll what? Joel is untouchable, and I won't be pushed into marrying someone I don't love—not even for you.'

'Since when has Joel Brent been untouchable? Besides, I know where he is right at this moment.'

Her look was sharp. 'You—you do?'

'Of course, he's in Scotland.'

She shook her head. 'He'll have left by now, he isn't stupid enough to stay there.'

'Nevertheless, he's still there. I have some one watching the cottage. Brent hasn't moved since he got back five minutes after you left.'

Five minutes—she had missed him by five minutes! But he was still there. If she could get back to him . . .

'No, Sabina,' her father cut in on her thoughts. 'You aren't going back to Scotland.'

'But if Joel's still there . . .'

He sighed. 'I don't want to have to get tough, Sabina, but——'

'Oh, get tough,' she invited tauntingly. 'By all means get tough.'

'Brent hasn't left Scotland because he obviously believes, for some reason, that you won't divulge his whereabouts to the press. Now if a story were to appear on him in the newspapers tomorrow he could come to only one conclusion—couldn't he?'

It was Sabina's turn to pale. 'You wouldn't?'

'I told you I'd get tough.'

'That's playing dirty, not getting tough. Dad, you couldn't do that to me?' she pleaded.

His shoulders slumped wearily. 'I have to, child. You won't have a bad life with Nicholas, I can promise you that. He'll never harm you.'

'Physically perhaps not, but what about mentally? What do you think it will do to me to be the wife of a man I don't love?'

'Does Brent want to marry you?' he asked cruelly.

'That wasn't kind,' she choked.

'I'm not trying to be kind,' he snapped. 'Just accept this interlude in Scotland for what it was.'

'And what was it?'

'A mutual need, maybe. Yes, that's it, that's what it must have been,' he said eagerly. 'You were feeling trapped, were just ripe for an affair, and I have it on good authority that Brent has been living in Scotland for the past eleven months, alone at that. And he was well known for his exploits with the fairer sex before he disappeared. I can understand how it happened, Sabina. I can even sympathise.'

'But it makes no difference?'

'It can't. I'm sorry, darling, really I am. But you don't mean anything to Brent, better to forget him.'

'And marry Nicholas!'

He sighed. 'Yes.'

'I'm going to bed,' she told him disgustedly, going to her bedroom door.

'And Nicholas?' He looked anxious. 'Will the wedding go ahead?'

'I don't know. I'm confused. I'll let you know in the morning.'

She had to think. Her father had revealed too many things this evening for her to be able to think straight. Putting together the fact that Joel would believe she had given his story to the newspapers, and her father's stupidity in taking money from Chasnick Enterprises, it would appear she had little choice.

And yet she still fought against her fate. What life could she possibly have married to Nicholas, a man she didn't love? And yet what life would any of them have if she didn't marry him? Her father would be ruined, probably publicly. And her father was too old to start again; the scandal could even kill him. Besides, what reason did she have not to marry Nicholas? There was no possibility of her ever being able to marry Joel, he had made his opinion of her perfectly clear.

What a thing to happen to her! And yet if she hadn't met Joel and fallen in love with him she might quite happily have married Nicholas. Oh, she had been getting nervous, but then most brides did this with their wedding so near. Yes, she might easily have married him if she hadn't met Joel, and now it appeared she had to.

'Well?' her father asked her over breakfast the next morning.

It was a breakfast that for Sabina consisted only of fresh orange juice, having no appetite for food. How different it would have been if she had still been with Joel and Satan, both of them tucking into hearty breakfasts while Satan patiently waited for any scraps that they left.

But she wasn't still in Scotland, and Joel was probably thinking that everything he had ever said about her was true. If only——

'Sabina?' her father prompted.

'Yes?' she asked coolly.

'You know very well what I'm asking. Good God, girl, I've hardly had any sleep all night just wondering what decision you're going to come to.'

He did look rather pale, but Sabina's heart remained hard against him. 'Am I supposed to feel sorry for you?'

He had the grace to look uncomfortable. 'What have you decided?'

Sabina stood up, a slim figure in close-fitting green trousers and a pale green silky blouse tucked in at her narrow waist. 'What I've decided should surely be told to Nicholas first?'

'But——'

'I'm sorry, Dad,' she cut in, 'but that's the way I feel.' She felt amost guilty about the anxiety he couldn't hide as they waited for Nicholas to arrive. But he should be made to suffer a little for what he was making her do.

They didn't have long to wait for Nicholas, he arrived shortly after ten, looking just as handsome and assured as he usually did. His grey checked trousers fitted snugly to his waist and thighs, the black silk shirt casually unbuttoned down his chest. His dark hair was brushed back from his face, the harshness of his face replaced with a softer emotion as he looked at Sabina.

'Darling,' he bent to kiss her, raising his eyebrows as his lips met the coolness of her cheek.

'Nicholas,' she greeted distantly. 'You're looking well.'

'So are you.' His arm went about her shoulders. 'These few days with your aunt seem to have done you good.'

'Thank you. Would you leave us, Dad?'

'But——'

'I think that might be a good idea, Charles,' Nicholas advised smoothly. 'Sabina and I have some talking to do.'

'We do indeed,' she agreed grimly.

'I'll be in my study,' her father said irritably. 'But as I don't have any work to do don't keep me in there all day.' He picked up the daily newspapers and left.

'So, Sabina,' Nicholas smiled. 'What——'

'Before you go any further,' she cut in, 'I think I should tell you that my father has borrowed money from Chasnick Enterprises.'

Nicholas wasn't in the least disconcerted by her disclosure. 'Yes?'

Sabina admired his calm, his assurance. 'You don't seem surprised.'

'I'm not,' he shrugged. 'I found out about it a few

months ago, but as you're going to be my wife . . .'

'I believe it was because of this money that my father agreed so readily to our marriage.'

'I shouldn't be at all surprised. He wouldn't be the businessman I know him to be if it wasn't.'

Sabina bit her lip. 'I'm still willing to marry you——'

'How nice,' he mocked.

'But I want it in writing that you'll forget my father's lapse, that no more will be said about it.' She held her breath as she waited for his answer.

Nicholas reached into his shirt pocket for his gold cigar case, slowly taking out one of the thin cigars he smoked, lighting it to blow smoke into the room. 'Why in writing?' He sat down, crossing one leg over the other as he looked at her.

'Because—because I don't intend having that held over my head every time you want to bring me into line. The marriage could only work if we enter into it on an equal footing.'

For a long time he was silent, gazing thoughtfully out of the window. Finally he turned to her. 'What if I don't agree?'

'Then I won't marry you.'

'You really mean that?'

It was a decision she had come to during the night, and it was one she had to stick to. Surely her father's long-standing partnership with Nicholas meant more to him than one breach of their contract on her father's part? 'Yes,' she told him firmly.

'Okay,' he shrugged, 'I'll agree to that. It's already been forgotten as far as I'm concerned.'

'The written agreement, when will I get that?'

'On our wedding day.'

'Oh,' she said dully.

Nicholas smiled, standing up to come over to her side.

'That was business, Sabina,' he told her huskily. 'And while you learn fast, I've been making deals for the last twenty-five years. I never make mistakes. I want to marry you, to look after you. So, do you promise to marry me?'

'Promise?'

'I know you never break your word.'

How strange that Nicholas should so readily take her word as being binding, whereas Joel had never trusted her, not even for a minute. 'I promise,' she smiled. 'Do we shake hands on the deal now?'

'No,' he laughed huskily. 'There are much better ways of clinching a deal with a beautiful woman.' He bent his head to kiss her.

The door to the study swung open with a bang. 'Sab—— Oh! Er—sorry.' Her father looked very embarrassed.

Nicholas gave him an impatient look. 'Don't you ever knock, Charles?'

'I thought I heard you leave.'

'No,' Nicholas's arm remained about Sabina's shoulders, 'Sabina and I were just discussing wedding arrangements. Right?' he looked down at her.

'Right,' she smiled gratefully, glad that he hadn't revealed to her father the extent of his knowledge concerning his borrowing.

Her father looked taken aback. 'Everything is—all right?' He looked confused.

'Everything is fine,' Sabina assured him. 'My holiday with—Aunt Daphne gave me a chance to think, away from the pressure of the wedding and everything.'

'I—— Good, good.' Her father looked relieved. 'These women!' he teased to Nicholas. 'They always make things so complicated.'

'Well, we just uncomplicated it, didn't we, darling?' He kissed Sabina lightly on the lips. 'The *Sunday Planet*,' he noticed the newspaper in Charles' hand. 'What are you doing reading a rival newspaper?' he taunted.

'I always read the competition. It seems we've missed out on an important story.' He was looking at Sabina as he spoke.

'The Joel Brent one?' Nicholas queried.

His partner nodded. 'You've seen it?'

'No. I did hear a whisper, though.'

Sabina was pale. 'What Joel Brent story?' she asked in a choked voice.

Nicholas looked down at her. 'Don't tell me you're a fan of his? I can't stand the man myself.'

'I—I like him.' Oh, what an understatement! She put her hand out for the newspaper her father still held. 'Let me see.'

He held back. 'I can tell you what it says. Brent's back in circulation. Apparently he's been working on new material for the past year, including a couple of film scores. But now he's back, starting with a concert at the Albert Hall next month.'

Sabina took the newspaper, moving away from her father and Nicholas, her heart beating erratically at the sight of Joel on the front page, the Joel she had come to love, the shaggy-haired, whipcord-lean man she had known in Scotland. And he was coming back to London.

CHAPTER FIVE

WHAT was she doing here? What had she been doing here every day this week? Waiting outside an auspicious place like the Albert Hall just trying to catch a glimpse of Joel was hardly the occupation she should have been following. There were still so many things to be done for the wedding—alterations to her dress, the final choice of flowers, and yet each day she could be found standing here, avidly searching the crowd for the sight of a tall dark-haired man with piercing grey eyes. She was searching for Joel Brent.

She had deduced from the newspaper article that if Joel was giving a concert then he would have to rehearse for it, hence her presence here. The rehearsals would have to be carried out at the Albert Hall itself, she knew that, and yet so far Joel hadn't been here. The concert was being given the next day, so surely he would have to come here today.

By six-thirty she turned dejectedly to go home. He wouldn't arrive now, she might as well leave. What could she say to him even if she did see him—more to the point, would he want to speak to her? She very much doubted it.

'Sabina.'

She lifted green eyes in a pale face, her heartbeat quickening, her mouth suddenly dry. She had been so deep in thought she hadn't seen him, hadn't noticed as he left the hall and walked purposefully towards her. 'Joel!' she breathed dazedly.

He looked different, dressed differently. In Scotland

he had been a rugged devil of a man, now he was
smoothly polished, his hair styled, the cream suit and
brown shirt he wore obviously expensive, by their cut.
And yet the wildness was still there, in the mockery of
his eyes and the sensuousness of his lips.

'Who else were you expecting?' he taunted now, that
cynical twist to his mouth.

Sabina shook her head, feeling all kinds of a fool for
her dazed behaviour. 'Expecting?' she repeated. 'I don't
understand.'

He took her elbow, leading her over to a car that had
miraculously appeared in front of them. He got into the
back beside her, issuing orders to the chauffeur. Grey
eyes raked mercilessly over her as the window between
them and the driver was electrically closed, giving them
complete privacy.

'Who else could you have been waiting for so dili-
gently the last five days?' he asked dryly.

She gasped her surprise. 'You knew I was outside?'

He nodded. 'I saw you the first day—and avoided
you. As I've avoided you every day since.'

'But—but why?'

'You ask me that?' he gave a harsh laugh. 'You ruined
things for me, girl, forced this life back on me before I
was ready for it. Oh, not that I'm not enjoying it,' he
smiled mockingly. 'Female company has never been so
plentiful, much more so than before.'

'And I'm sure that worries you!' she flashed, staring
out of the car window.

'It does,' he grinned. 'I couldn't possibly hope to cope
with all the offers from beautiful blondes I've had. I
know my limitations.'

'I didn't know you had any!' Her imagination was
working overtime as she wondered how many women
he had slept with since his return to London.

He gave a careless shrug. 'One woman a night is enough for me.' He sat forward suddenly, reaching out for her left hand. The diamond and emerald ring sparkled on her third finger. 'Is one man now enough for you?' he asked insultingly.

Sabina snatched her hand away, glaring at him. 'I hate you!' she told him vehemently.

'I'm sure you do,' he taunted. 'I ruined your big story for you, didn't I, coming back like this? I knew as soon as you disappeared that I'd have to get things moving quicker than I'd anticipated. The concert took some organising at such short notice, I can tell you. Although a lot of it was already in the pipeline. I'd always planned to come back, you see, I just took time off because the publicity after the accident sickened me. But my time in Scotland was never meant to be a permanent thing.'

Her eyes were wide. 'You always planned to come back?' she repeated dazedly.

'But in my own time. I hate to admit it, but I was really beginning to trust you that last day in Scotland. So much for trust,' he added bitterly.

'You don't think I left because I wanted to?'

'Why else?' he scorned. 'The first time I left you alone you disappeared. After ransacking my home, of course.' Anger entered his voice. 'If I'd laid hands on you again that day you'd have got a sound beating.'

'But——'

'Wait until we get inside,' he ordered. The car had come to a halt and Joel pushed her out on to the pavement.

They weren't at Sabina's home but were parked outside another block of flats, these ones looking even more exclusive than her own. 'Where are we?' she asked nervously.

'Where do you think?' he mocked.

The penthouse apartment was everything it should be, big, luxurious, expensively furnished—and totally lacking in homely warmth. Except for a black bundle of fur audaciously curled up on one of the leather chairs.

'Satan!' Sabina rushed forward to greet him.

At the first sound of her voice the cat's eyes opened, his black ears pricked up. He jumped down from the chair, purring loudly, rubbing into Sabina's hand as she stroked him.

'Oh, Satan,' she choked, picking him up in her arms and cuddling into his silky fur. She looked at Joel with tears in her eyes. 'You brought him with you!'

'Obviously,' he drawled.

'But you said he went with the cottage, that he stayed there.'

Joel shrugged. 'He didn't seem to want to stay. Especially after you left. He missed you,' he added softly.

'I've missed him too,' she smiled tearfully.

'So I can see. So I brought him with me. The only trouble is he hates it here.'

'Of course he does. He needs to live in a house, somewhere out in the country.'

'I know that,' Joel said tersely. 'I just haven't had time to go about looking for a house.'

'Perhaps I could——' She broke off her eager words, biting painfully into her bottom lip.

'Perhaps you could what?' He watched her with narrowed eyes. 'I hope you weren't going to suggest looking for one for me?'

Her head went back proudly. 'You said you don't have the time.'

'I'll make time.'

'When?'

'As soon as I can,' he said irritably.

'That isn't good enough. Satan needs to be out in the fresh air again, free to roam.' She continued to cuddle the cat.

'I know that,' Joel snapped. 'Perhaps you have some leaflets on houses I can look at? When is the wedding— two weeks now, isn't it?'

'Yes,' she agreed shortly. 'And Nicholas and I aren't moving into a house. It's much more convenient to live in his flat.'

'For him, maybe. But how do you feel about it?'

Sabina flushed. 'It will be convenient for me too,' she told him tightly.

'Are you going to continue working after you're married?'

'Working? But I—— No,' she suddenly realised what he meant. 'No, I'm not.'

'That's a shame—for them, I mean. When are you going to give me back the things you took from the cottage?' he demanded suddenly.

Sabina looked bewildered. 'What things?'

'Letters, photographs, some of my music sheets.'

Mike! That man Mike had stayed in the cottage several minutes after she had gone to the car. He had put something in the boot of the car, but at the time she had assumed it to be her rucksack. Now she knew he had put some other things in there too. And Joel thought that she had taken them!

'I don't have them,' she told him dully, sitting down with Satan still in her arms.

'I don't suppose you do. I presume them to be somewhere at the newspaper office. But if one of those photographs or letters appears in any newspaper I shall sue. Tell that to your fiancé.'

'Joel, I—' she looked at him pleadingly, 'I didn't

take them. You see, two men came to the cottage, and they——'

'Oh yes,' he sat down too, his expression taunting, 'and I suppose they kidnapped you?'

'More or less. You see——'

'Your acting is still very good,' he told her harshly. 'Fortunately I'm still immune to it. And while I may have found your blonde-haired, green-eyed beauty appealing in Scotland, the same doesn't apply here. There are too many women in London, with exactly the same to offer, and you just aren't worth the trouble involved. Now,' he said hardly, 'I want those things back. They were—personal things, certainly not for the eyes of a little story-hunter like you.'

'Please, Joel——'

'I want them back, Sabina. I wouldn't even be talking to you now if it weren't for them. I'm not in the habit of associating with thieves.'

'I didn't take your belongings!' She gave him a sharp look. 'Were the letters from Nicole Dupont?'

He looked down his arrogant nose at her. 'And if they were?'

'Love letters?' she choked.

'You should know, you've read them, you and a couple of dozen other people by now.'

'I don't have them,' she repeated. 'But I know who does.'

'Well?' he snapped.

She took a deep breath. 'The two men, the ones who came to the cottage, they took them. Now I don't know where they are, but——'

'Don't lie to me, Sabina!' He pulled her to her feet, his fingers digging into her flesh. 'You—— Ouch!' he flinched away as Satan's claws struck out and scratched his hand. 'My God!' he sucked the blood from the

wound. 'I wasn't going to hurt her, you stupid animal!'
he glared at the cat.

Sabina held back a smile, remembering his lack of
sympathy when the same thing had happened to her.
'He was only protecting me,' she pointed out.

Joel scowled. 'He should have been protecting *me*.'
He turned on his heel, opening a door and entering
another room.

She followed him, standing in the doorway as he took
a bottle out of the bathroom cabinet. 'What are you
doing?' she asked with feigned innocence.

'Antiseptic,' he growled.

' "Cats are very clean animals",' she told him mockingly.

'Very funny,' he snapped. 'It damn well stings!' He
rubbed some of the ointment on to the gash.

'I know.' She was having great difficulty holding back
her amusement, especially as Satan could now be heard
purring loudly in the background.

'Okay, okay, so I should have had more sympathy
with you. That cat is vicious!'

'He just didn't like seeing you attack me.' She was
smiling openly now.

'I wasn't attacking you. I'm just sick and tired of this
act you put on all the time. Believe me, being Mrs
Nicholas Freed isn't worth it.'

Her amusement instantly died, her eyes shadowed. 'I'll
find out where the two men live, and get your things
back.' Her voice was stilted. 'Take care of Satan for
me.'

She should never have tried to see Joel, she had just
made marrying Nicholas all the harder to bear. But she
had made Nicholas a promise, and she couldn't break
that. Besides, Nicholas was being wonderful about the
whole thing, acting as if the conversation had never

taken place, and so making things much less strained for her.

'Sabina . . .' Joel was frowning, watching her closely, 'are you frightened of Freed?'

'No,' she gave a bright smile. 'No, of course not.'

'These two men,' he said thoughtfully. 'Did he send them looking for you?'

'No,' she answered truthfully. 'I—I'm sorry you had your belongings taken. I'm sure my—I'm sure that wasn't supposed to happen.' For some reason she still didn't want him to know who her father was, maybe because she felt that would damn her for all time in his eyes.

'You mean there really were two men?' he frowned.

She nodded. 'You remember the man you thought was attracted to me at the hotel?'

'Those two?' He watched as she gave a confirming nod. 'No wonder they couldn't take their eyes off you. But if Freed didn't send them, who did?'

'I have to go now. I—I'm expected back for dinner.' Oh, how she longed to stay here. Everything she cared about was in this room, the man she loved, the cat who would protect her even from his own master.

'Back where?' Joel's eyes were narrowed.

'Home.'

'With Freed?'

She blushed. 'We aren't married yet.'

'And that makes a difference?' he scorned.

'Of course,' she snapped. 'Now I really do have to go. I'll let you know about those things as soon as I have them.'

He grabbed her arm. 'No, Satan!' he ordered as the cat looked ready to spring again. He sighed. 'Reassure your protector, will you?'

Sabina smoothed the black silky fur, feeling the tension going out of the whipcord body. 'I think he's all right now,' she smiled.

'All right!' Joel dismissed disgustedly. 'The animal's enslaved. You should take him. Does Freed like cats?'

She looked startled. 'I—I don't know. I've never asked him.'

'On second thoughts perhaps it isn't such a good idea. If Freed can knock a woman about he could certainly ill-treat an animal.' He frowned. 'If you aren't going back to Freed who are you going back to?'

She had flinched at his mention of Nicholas's treatment of his last wife, but now she held her head proudly erect. 'Perhaps I live alone,' she suggested distantly.

Joel shook his head. 'You said you were expected back.'

This man was altogether too astute. 'I live with my father. Is that respectable enough for you?'

'That depends.'

'On what?'

'On who he is.'

Sabina gave a casual shrug. 'He's just my father,' she made her tone as nonchalant as she could. 'Good luck with the concert tomorrow.'

'Aren't you coming?'

'Are you kidding?' she laughed. 'Tickets are like gold dust.'

'It's a sell-out,' he admitted. 'But I could get you in if you wanted to come.'

'No! I—er—I don't think Nicholas—I don't think he——'

'The invitation didn't include him,' Joel said harshly.

'He wouldn't let me go without him.'

'Maybe you're right not to want to go with him. He's a little old for that type of entertainment. Okay, Sabina. I'll expect to hear from you.'

'Yes.' She was strangely reluctant to leave, and yet she knew she had to go. As it was she was late back and Nicholas had already arrived, he and her father discussing business while she changed.

Nicholas handed her a Martini when she joined them, her black dress giving her a look of cool sophistication. It was the way Nicholas liked her to look, and since her return from Scotland she had tried her best to please him, even accepting his light lovemaking without demur.

She could hardly wait for the evening to end, wanting to talk to her father, kissing Nicholas a distracted goodbye before hurrying back into the lounge. Her father's eyebrows rose as she made her request for the full names and addresses of the men Ray and Mike.

'What on earth—— Why the hell should you want to know that?' he demanded curiously.

'You know the reason,' she told him impatiently. 'You had no right to take anything that belonged to Joel. They work for you, so you can get the things back.'

'What things?' He looked genuinely puzzled.

'Don't pretend with me, Dad. We've gone past the need for that. Joel wants his possessions returned to him, and I intend to see that he gets them.'

'You've seen Brent?'

Sabina blushed. 'Yes.' She avoided his eyes.

'If Nicholas should find out——'

'He won't,' she told him firmly.

'Can't you stay away from the man?' her father said irritably. 'Good grief, girl, don't you realise the risk you're taking?'

'Don't worry, your reputation is perfectly safe. As soon as I have Nicholas's wedding ring on my finger you can breathe easily again.'

'I wish you understood—— No, you can't. But I'm only

doing what I think is best, Sabina, for you. I just wish you wouldn't be so bitter about it.'

She sighed. 'I don't mean to be. But you will get those things back, won't you? Joel thinks I took them, and I——'

'If you tell me what things you mean I'll do my best,' he interrupted.

Her eyes widened. 'You mean you really don't know?'

'Doesn't my complete mystification tell you that?'

'But they work for you,' she frowned.

'I just told them to get you back, nothing else interested me about that setup.'

'Then I think you should have a little talk with the one called Mike, he brought more than me back with him.'

'I see,' he nodded. 'I'll look into it.'

Sabina hoped he did more than that. She would hate Mike to actually use the things he took. And Joel would certainly never forgive her.

Nicholas took her shopping the next afternoon, insisting on buying her a new dress. 'I'm taking you somewhere special tonight,' he explained.

'Where?' she asked dully, wishing she could have gone to Joel's concert. But not with Nicholas! That would never do, she would only give herself away. Nicholas was far from stupid, and he wouldn't be able to miss her complete absorption in the man on the stage.

'Wait and see,' he patted her gently on the cheek. 'Try the green one on,' he advised as the assistant brought out three dresses for her to look at.

He often chose her clothes for her, having superb taste, and she wondered whether he had gained this knowledge by choosing his other wife's clothes. She never used to think about Nancy Freed, had just accepted that the marriage hadn't been a success, but now she found herself wondering more and more about the other woman, about what she was like, whether she had found it impossible to fall in love with Nicholas too.

She tried the dress on mechanically, knowing its sheath-like style suited her, its knee-length showing her shapely legs and slender ankles. If only she were dressing up for Joel!

'We'll take that one,' Nicholas told the saleswoman.

The way he didn't even ask Sabina if she liked it rankled, but she raised no protest, giving it to the woman to put in a box, knowing by her smile that it was an expensive dress. Sabina didn't care, she didn't care about anything any more. Two weeks from today she would be Nicholas's wife, and then he would have the right to choose all her clothes for her.

'You're very thoughtful today,' he remarked on the drive back to her home.

She couldn't stop thinking about Joel, about what he was doing, the people he was with, the *women* he was with. Would it be a dark-haired beauty with flashing blue eyes like Nicole Dupont, or a redhead, or possibly a blonde like herself? Yes, it would be a blonde, he said he had a weakness for them.

'Sabina?' Nicholas prompted.

'Sorry.' She forced herself to smile at him. 'I—I was just wondering where the "somewhere special" could be you're taking me to tonight,' she invented.

'I'll guarantee you'll enjoy it. Just think, Sabina, two weeks from today we'll be man and wife.'

She was trying not to think of it, her emotions numb concerning the wedding and the events that would follow it. Now if the bridegroom had been Joel . . .

'Sabina?' Nicholas's tone was sharp now.

'I—— Sorry,' she blushed. 'I——'

'Are you having second thoughts again?' he asked suspiciously.

'No, of course not——'

His hand moved to cover hers as it rested in her lap. 'Sure?'

She couldn't meet the look in his eyes. 'Yes.'

'Okay,' he sighed. 'I'll call for you at seven and we'll have an early dinner. We have to be somewhere by eight-thirty.'

Like all women she felt a burning curiosity to know where they would be going. 'You're very mysterious,' she probed.

He just laughed, dropping her off at her home before going to his flat to change. Her father was at home when she got in, and wordlessly handed her a thick brown envelope.

She took a look inside. Letters, photographs, and music sheets! 'You got them back!' Her eyes glowed.

'In the end,' he nodded. 'Mike wasn't too happy about returning them.'

Sabina looked worried. 'You're sure they're all here?'

'He says they are.'

'But are they?'

Her father shrugged. 'Only Brent can tell you that.'

'Yes, yes, of course.' These things would give her an excuse to see Joel again. If she needed an excuse!

'I think you should post them to him,' her father advised, seeming to read her thoughts.

Sabina clutched the envlope to her. 'I don't know his address, only where his apartment is.'

'I'm sure I could find out the address for you.'

'No! I—I'll take them to him.'

'Is your affair with him still going on?' her father demanded to know.

Sabina flushed. 'There was no affair,' she told him tightly.

'But you told me—were you lying about sleeping with him?'

She sighed. 'I never said I had. I told you we shared a bedroom, and that's all we did.'

'Well, I'll be damned!'

'You probably will be,' she said dully. 'We probably both will be. Me for marrying a man I don't love, and you for letting me.'

'Sabina, if you really don't want to marry him I'm sure we can work something out. I just think you'll be happy with Nicholas. He's strong and dependable. Your future with him will be secure. But if you really don't want to I——'

'It doesn't matter, Dad,' she dismissed briskly. 'Now I have to get ready or I shall be late. Do you have any idea where Nicholas is taking me?'

'None at all. But try and enjoy yourself, hmm, child. Nicholas obviously thinks you're going to like it, wherever it is.'

She slowly prepared for her date with Nicholas, having a leisurely bath, her skin feeling smooth and soft from the perfumed oil she had added to the water. Her hair she left long and straight, newly washed, the colour of pure gold.

When she at last surveyed herself in the full-length mirror in her room she knew Nicholas would have no reason to fault her appearance. The green gown was the colour of her eyes, the figure-hugging style emphasising every curve of her body as if it loved it. She wore high black sandals, the high heels emphasising the slenderness of ankle and calf.

Yes, she looked coolly beautiful, and Nicholas would be pleased with the result. If only she could have loved

Nicholas! She was aware that she had agreed to marry him in the first place because it had seemed to be what everyone wanted, including herself at the time.

If only this could have been one of those romantic novels she so enjoyed reading, where the heroine fell in love with the man she was forced to marry! But then those girls weren't usually in love with another man, and the man they had to marry wasn't usually old enough to be their father. By the time she was twenty-five Nicholas would be in his fifties.

His blue eyes deepened with appreciation as soon as he saw her, and he bent his dark head to kiss her lightly on the lips. 'You're growing up, Sabina,' he said huskily.

It wasn't what she had expected him to say, and yet it echoed her own thoughts. She was *having* to grow up, and quickly. 'Is that a compliment?' she asked teasingly.

Nicholas smiled. 'You know it was.' He looked at his wrist-watch. 'We'd better get moving. I have a table booked for seven-fifteen. Lord, what an uncivilised time to dine!' he grimaced.

'Am I allowed to know where we're going now?' she asked once they were in the car on their way to the restaurant.

He grinned. 'I take back what I said about you being grown up, at the moment you look very like an eager child.' He squeezed her hands. 'You're beautiful, Sabina. I can't tell you how proud I am that you're going to be my wife.'

She bit back a bitter retort. She was grateful to him for saving her father's feelings, but surely he must realise that if it weren't for that—and her father's threat to do a story on Joel!—that she wouldn't be marrying him at all? Yes, he knew, he just chose to ignore it.

'You still haven't told me,' she reminded him.

'So I haven't. Well, the other day you told me that you're a fan of Joel Brent's, and while I can't stand the man myself, I want to please you.'

Sabina had gone pale. 'You haven't——?'

'I have,' Nicholas told her triumphantly. 'I have the best seats in the house. Plus,' he paused for effect, 'I've got us an invitation to the party being given afterwards in Brent's honour. Now what do you think of that?'

CHAPTER SIX

WHAT did she think of it? What could she think of it!
She thought of nothing else as she tried to make a pretence of eating her dinner, trying to look happy with the
arrangements Nicholas had made for their evening,
when all the time she was wondering how she would be
able to bear it.

She had put on a brave face after his announcement,
pretending delight with his surprise for her. He was
trying to please her, doing his best to make her happy.
He couldn't possibly know he had chosen the one way
to make her *un*happy.

How could she sit in that hall and watch all those
other women falling for Joel's sensual magnetism, hear
all those other women screaming and showing their
adoration as he played upon that adulation to the full?
He was an expert at it, she had seen him do it before;
he used his body as well as his voice to capture his
audience.

When the time came to enter the hall she almost
turned tail and ran, only the thought of Nicholas's
questions if she should do such a thing making her stay
at his side. The place was huge, and not one she was
used to frequenting, therefore the closeness of their seats
to the stage Joel would shortly walk on to came as
something of a shock to her. They were only feet away
from where he would stand!

'All right?' Nicholas leant towards her, entwining
his fingers with hers.

'Yes—lovely,' she answered jerkily, longing to take

her hand away from his.

When the lights finally went down and the orchestra began to play Sabina thought she was going to faint. And then Joel walked on to the stage in front of her, just out of the darkness, his dazzling smile capturing every female present—including Sabina. The concert was being televised, the cameras unobtrusive, but there nonetheless. But Joel was playing only to the audience before him, silencing the orchestra after the applause had died down, standing alone in the spotlight as he sang only to the accompaniment of a guitar the soft love song that had taken him to the top of the charts two years ago.

Sabina was mesmerised from that first song, sitting immobile as the rest of the audience applauded him. All she could think of, all she could see, was how truly magnificent Joel looked, the black evening suit tailored on to him, the snowy white shirt with its frilly front not in the least effeminate when worn by such a ruggedly handsome man.

At the end of this ovation he launched into a medley of songs that soon had the audience joining in, clapping and shouting their enjoyment. Sabina sat silently through it all, and if Nicholas spoke to her she certainly never heard him, having eyes and ears only for Joel.

This was where he belonged, where he truly came alive. And his voice, his beautiful sexy voice—what spells it wove, how it enmeshed the heart, stirred the senses. When the interval came Sabina wasn't even aware of it for several minutes; she felt totally dazed.

'I never realised you were such a fan of his,' Nicholas remarked at her side.

She blinked into realisation of her surroundings. 'Sorry . . .?'

'You've been lost to me for the last hour.'

'I'm sorry,' she forced herself to smile. 'He was good, wasn't he?' What an understatement!

'Very,' Nicholas agreed dryly, obviously not sharing her pleasure. 'I'm glad you're enjoying it. Care to come outside for a bit?'

'I—— No, I think I'll stay here.' She wasn't sure her legs would hold her.

'I'll make sure you're back in your seat for the second half,' he teased.

Again she smiled, a totally mechanical action, because he seemed to expect it of her. 'I'd rather stay here—if you don't mind, that is?'

'Of course not,' he agreed readily. 'I'm just going for a smoke, all right?'

'Yes—yes, fine.'

Sabina felt strangely vulnerable when he had gone, jumping with surprise when someone tapped her on the shoulder. The man in front of her looked as if he worked here, by his uniform.

'Miss Smith?' he enquired.

'Yes?' She sounded puzzled.

'I was told to give you this.' He handed her a slip of paper.

'It isn't Nicholas, is it?' Panic entered her voice. 'Nothing has happened to him, has it?'

He shrugged. 'I'm sorry, Miss Smith, but I don't know anyone called Nicholas. I was just asked to give you that note.'

Joel! This note was from *Joel*. She unfolded the square of paper with shaking fingers. The message was short and abrupt. He wanted to see her, now, backstage.

'I—er—Mr Brent—— He——'

'You're to come with me, Miss Smith,' the man told her quietly. 'That is, if you want to.'

'Oh yes!' Her eyes glowed and she clutched the note

to her, standing up to follow him. She walked behind the man in a daze, finally finding herself standing outside a door.

'Just knock, miss,' the man advised. 'He's expecting you.'

Her knock was timid, hardly loud enough to be heard, and yet almost before her hand had left contact with the wood the door was flung open. Joel looked no less impressive this close to, if anything he looked even more so.

'Come in,' he pulled her roughly inside. 'We'll talk later, Lennie,' he spoke to the man just inside the room.

Sabina didn't even look at him, her gaze was riveted on Joel, on the sensual vitality of him, the sex-appeal that still oozed out of him. Her attention was so entranced she couldn't even have given a vague description of Lennie if someone had asked her for one.

'We don't have time for later, Joel,' Lennie insisted. 'You can't just decide to scrap the last number.'

'I just did it,' he was told firmly. 'Tell Nigel not to play it.'

'But, Joel——'

'Tell him, Lennie.' The poor man was pushed pointedly towards the door. 'I'm busy.'

Lennie looked impatiently at Sabina. 'You have five minutes, Joel, and then you have to be back on stage, girl-friend or no girl-friend.'

Joel's mouth twisted. 'Miss Smith is not my *girl-friend*,' he declared scornfully.

The other man shrugged. 'About this last number——'

'I told you, Lennie, *scrap it*.'

'But it's your new release!'

'So they'll all hear it on the radio. I am not singing it tonight! Got it?'

'Got it,' the other man accepted with ill grace, and left the room with a slam of the door.

'Who was he?' Sabina asked huskily.

'My manager,' Joel told her tersely.

Her eyes widened. 'And you treated him like that?'

Grey eyes narrowed on her. 'The way I treat my manager is none of your affair,' he snapped. 'Now what the hell are you doing here tonight? And with Freed!'

'I would have thought that was obvious—we came to hear you sing,' she retorted, stung by his cold manner.

'I'm sure Freed has no real wish to hear me sing,' he scorned.

'But I did.'

'You said you wouldn't be coming,' he reminded her moodily.

'Nicholas wanted to surprise me.'

'He didn't only surprise you. I had the shock of my life when I saw you sitting in the audience.'

Her interest quickened. 'And when did you see me?'

'As soon as I came out on stage.'

'I would never have guessed it,' she said breathlessly.

'Very few women have that silver-blonde hair,' he dismissed with cool indifference.

'I'm surprised you noticed amongst all those screaming women,' she snapped.

'Is it my imagination or are your eyes more green than usual?' he taunted.

'Not over you they aren't! I have better things to do with my time than drool over some ageing sex-symbol.' Her words were deliberately insulting.

His face tautened, his eyes glittered dangerously. '*I'm* old? My God, what about the man you've been holding hands with the last hour? Now *that's* what I call old!'

'Nicholas is in his prime!' she defended.

'He's nothing but a dirty old man,' Joel dismissed

scathingly. 'I despise his type intensely. And I despise
the girls who get involved with men like him.' His gaze
ran over her insolently. 'He keeps you dressed well,
anyway. I presume he did buy that expensive creation
you're wearing?' The colour that flooded her face gave
him his answer. 'Some girls enjoy being bought,' he
sneered. 'But marriage is rather a high price to pay,
even for a man like Freed.'

It was obvious he believed her to be a girl intent on
marrying a man for his money. 'A price you aren't willing to pay,' Sabina said tautly. 'Not after killing the
woman you wanted to marry.' She paled at the blazing
anger in his face. 'Oh, my God, I'm sorry! I'm sorry,
Joel, I didn't mean that,' she pleaded.

'Get out of here,' he ordered icily. 'Get out!'

'Please, Joel,' she rushed to his side, her eyes implor-
ing. 'I didn't mean to say that. I—— Oh, God, what can I
say?' Tears flooded her eyes.

'Just get out.' His hands were clenched at his sides, his
knuckles white. 'I've been expecting some comments like
that ever since I came back, but I never thought you
would be the one to say them.'

'I didn't mean it!' she choked on her tears. 'Joel, I
didn't mean it!'

'I have to get back on stage.' He pulled his jacket
back on, looking at her with cold eyes. 'I would advise
you to go back to your seat, I'm sure Freed will oblig-
ingly hold your hand again.'

She hadn't even been aware that he had been doing
so the first time! 'Will you just let me——'

'You've said enough,' he told her harshly, as he left
the dressing-room, ready to face his audience once
again.

Sabina knew herself to be dismissed, and went
miserably back to her seat.

'Where have you been?' Nicholas demanded as she sat down.

'I—er—I decided to stretch my legs after all. I must have missed you in the crowd.' She couldn't look at him, her eyes still full of tears.

He seemed satisfied with her explanation. 'You're looking a little pale, darling,' he remarked concernedly.

'Just a headache,' she dismissed.

'Do you want to leave?'

'No!' She willed herself to act calm. She smiled. 'I don't want to miss any of the concert.'

'I know he's good, but——'

The audience suddenly erupted into applause as Joel came back on stage, smiling with just a hint of wickedness, none of his anger of a few minutes ago in evidence. Sabina learnt during the next hour and a half that Joel was a good actor; his burning anger during the interval was certainly genuine, although it was no longer evident in the dazzling performance he gave on stage.

Sabina couldn't really appreciate the second half, feeling too contrite to do any more than wish to speak to Joel at the earliest opportunity. She had to make him understand that she hadn't meant what she had said, that she had just been hitting out in anger. She knew that he hadn't deliberately hurt Nicole Dupont, knew it, and yet she had still accused him. She had to apologise, make him understand that she had only hit out at him because he had been hurting her.

At last the concert seemed to be coming to an end, the lights once again dimming to a single spotlight as a guitar began to play. A look of anger crossed Joel's face, and he turned to glare at someone behind him. Knowing of the argument he had had with his manager Sabina could only assume that the man Lennie had gone against Joel's wishes and had kept in the song he had wanted scrapped.

Joel's anger was quickly masked and could probably only be seen by the first couple of rows of people, most of whom would have no idea it had been anger. Except Sabina!

Finally Joel seemed to shrug, moving right to the front of the stage and sitting down on the top step of the stairs that led up the middle of the stage.

He was only feet away from Sabina, almost near enough to touch. And how she longed to touch him, yearned for the closeness they had been approaching in Scotland. Suddenly he looked up, straight at her, the blaze of contempt in his grey eyes making her recoil in her seat. God, she thought, he *hated* her!

And then he began to sing, more beautifully than Sabina had ever heard him sing before, his voice deep and husky, every word seeming to come from the heart. Sabina was held as enrapt as everyone else seemed to be.

> She came to my life in summer,
> The sunlight in her hair,
> But she went away, and took the sun with her,
> Yes, she's the girl who went away.

> The girl no man can hold,
> No matter how much he loves her.

> Why she went away I'll never know,
> Perhaps she couldn't love me,
> As I'll love her until the day I die,
>   if I'm not dead already;
> She's the girl who went away.

> The girl no man can hold,

No matter how much he loves her.

If ever you come back, summer girl,
I'll be waiting for you, longing for you
Then you'll stay, in my arms, in my heart,
And you'll no longer be the girl who went away.

The girl no man can hold,
No matter how much he loves her,
God, how I love you . . .

As the last haunting guitar chord died away there was complete silence in the hall, and then the thunderous applause broke out, people everywhere standing up, the highest accolade any singer could possibly have. And Joel deserved every minute of it.

He seemed as affected by the song as everyone else, taking several minutes to acknowledge the audience's reaction. Finally he managed to silence them. 'I want to thank you all for coming here tonight. And I thank you for liking my song. It was written for a very special girl, a girl who no longer exists. Thank you.'

There were cries of 'Encore!' and Joel took bow after bow, finally giving in to the demand of the audience and singing one more song. Sabina was aware of none of it, sitting beside Nicholas in silent misery. 'The girl who went away' was obviously a song about Nicole Dupont. How Joel must have loved her, must still love her! The emotion had been raw in his voice, the desolation, the loneliness 'of being without the woman he loved. And she had accused him of killing her! No wonder he had looked at her with unconcealed hatred.

She and Nicholas filed out of the hall with the rest of the people, hearing all around them words of pleasure and enjoyment, the praise for the one-man show they had just seen.

'As you have a headache shall we give the party a miss?' Nicholas's arm rested protectively about her shoulders, as he steered her towards their waiting car.

'No!' She spoke more sharply than she intended, giving a bright smile to cover her mood of depression. 'I may never get another chance to meet Joel Brent,' she added teasingly, knowing she had never spoken a truer word. After the things she had said to Joel during the show's interval she didn't think he would want to to see her ever again.

Nicholas shrugged. 'He's nothing special. He and Nancy, my ex-wife, had a thing going a few years back.'

Sabina's eyes widened. Joel certainly hadn't told her that! 'I—I didn't know.' She didn't look at Nicholas, afraid he might see the jealousy in her face and misconstrue it, think that it was over him and not over Joel.

'It didn't last long,' he said coldly. 'Maybe he found her as unfaithful as I did.'

Colour flooded Sabina's cheeks. 'We've never spoken of your other marriages, Nicholas,' she voiced hesitantly. 'Why didn't your marriage to Nancy work out?'

His expression was grim. 'Partly for the reason I've just told you.'

And partly because Nicholas had become violent! Not that he was likely to admit to that. 'I see.' She bit her lip.

He pulled her to his side, smiling down at her. 'We won't have any of those problems, Sabina. Our marriage will work out just fine.'

Until he decided to trade her in for a newer model. Each of his wives seemed to be younger than the last. 'Yes, Nicholas,' she replied obediently, sincerely hoping her attraction would be of short duration.

The party for Joel was being given in a private room

at one of the leading hotels in London, and the room
was full of celebrities from the stage and television.
Sabina saw Joel as soon as they entered the room, and
jealousy coursed through her for the black-haired beauty
clinging to his arm.

'Oh, hell!' she heard Nicholas mutter angrily.

She looked at him curiously. 'Is there anything
wrong?'

He scowled. 'The woman with Brent—that's Nancy.'

Sabina looked at the woman with new eyes, seeing a
woman of about thirty, possibly thirty-two, her black hair
cut almost as short as a man's, her make-up dramatically
dark, her red dress deliberately provocative. She was a
beautiful woman, very sophisticated, but there was a
discontented droop to her pouting red lips. Suddenly
she smiled up at Joel, and the unhappiness seemed to
leave her, her face becoming animated, her blue eyes
sparkling.

Sabina's breath caught in her throat. 'She's very
lovely,' she said dully, watching the way Joel smiled
back at the woman, an intimate smile, the sort he had
never given her.

'Yes,' Nicholas acknowledged tersely. 'Are you sure
you want to stay?'

She knew he wanted to leave, and yet she wanted to
see Joel, to talk to him, to apologise to him. 'You don't
even have to speak to your ex-wife if you don't want
to,' she reasoned. 'Besides, it's years since you were
divorced.'

His scowl became even darker. 'I'd rather leave,
Sabina. Oh, damn, she's seen us. She's coming over!'

'Calm down, Nicholas,' Sabina advised. 'Surely after
all this time you can at least greet each other politely?'

'You don't understand——'

'Nicholas!' Nancy Freed's voice was husky and attractive, her smile now somewhat brittle. 'How lovely to see you again.'

His face was set, his blue eyes cold. 'Is it?' he asked tightly.

Sabina had never seen him like this before, so tense, a pulse beating erratically at his jawline. 'Aren't you going to introduce us, Nicholas?' she pointedly reminded him of his manners.

'Of course. Sabina, Nancy. Nancy, this is Sabina Smith.'

It had hardly been much of an introduction, and she could see the other woman looking at her curiously.

'*The* Sabina Smith?' Nancy drawled.

'My fiancée, yes,' Nicholas nodded curtly.

'Oh, I didn't mean that,' Nancy dismissed impatiently. 'You're Charles's daughter, aren't you?' she spoke to Sabina.

'Do you know my father?' Sabina asked politely.

'I knew him when I was married to Nicholas. Come and join us, Joel,' she grabbed his arm as he stood talking to someone a few feet away. 'You know Nicholas, of course. And this is his fiancée, his partner's daughter.'

'Partner?' Joel frowned, not once looking at Sabina.

'Charles Smith. Surely you knew they were partners?' Nancy laughed.

'Probably, but I'd forgotten.' Joel at last looked at Sabina, the contempt even more evident than it had been earlier on the stage. 'Nice to meet you, Miss Smith,' he drawled mockingly.

'Mr Brent,' she replied coolly. 'I enjoyed your show tonight,' she told him with enthusiasm.

'Oh, were you there?' Nancy smiled at her. 'Lucky you, Sabina. Nicholas would never go to shows when we were married.'

'Not the sort of shows you wanted to go to,' her ex-husband snapped.

Nancy flushed. 'I was young and inexperienced.'

'I know that,' Nicholas snapped again. 'All you were interested in was——'

'So you're Charles Smith's daughter,' Joel spoke quietly at Sabina's side, taking her attention away from the conversation between ex-husband and wife, a conversation that looked like developing into an argument.

Sabina turned to look at him, aware that Nicholas and Nancy's conversation was becoming heated already. 'That's right,' she acknowledged huskily.

'Why didn't you tell me that?' His eyes were narrowed.

She shrugged. 'I didn't think you would be interested.'

'Like hell you didn't! So was it Freed or your father who sent you up to Scotland?'

'Neither,' she sighed. 'I've already explained why I was there.'

'But you're still engaged to him, still going to marry him,' Joel scorned.

Sabina looked away. 'Yes,' she agreed quietly.

'Why?'

Her eyes widened. 'Why do you think?'

'I have no idea.' He pulled her farther away from the other couple. 'You don't love Freed, and you don't seem to need his money either. So why marry him?'

'Why shouldn't I?' She threw her head back challengingly.

'Why indeed?' he agreed. 'What was Scotland all about, a last fling before you settle down to married life?'

'Something like that.' She evaded his eyes.

'And I was going to be the affair, I suppose,' he

mocked. 'Pity I wouldn't play. You really didn't know who I was when you arrived, did you?'

'No,' she confirmed. 'I—I have your letters and things back, by the way.'

'They were your father's men?'

'Mm,' Sabina nodded. 'He had them out looking for me. They traced me to that hotel, searched the area and couldn't find any further news of me. They were just about to give up when they spotted me with you in the bar.'

'You sound as if you wish they hadn't.' Joel was watching her closely.

'Yes,' she admitted. 'I—I liked being there with you.'

'Even though you're still going to marry Freed?' he said harshly.

'Yes. Would you like me to bring your things round tomorrow?' She hoped her pleading didn't show in her eyes. She so much wanted to see him, to be with him.

'What would be the point? I'm sure they've had copies made.'

'Oh no! You really think they have?' It was something that hadn't even occurred to her.

He nodded. 'No doubt about it. But you can tell your father that the same rule applies—just one letter, one photograph, and he'll find himself up against a law-suit. The newspapers had their fun with me a year ago, this time I'll fight anything they care to print.'

Sabina bit her lip, uncaring of the pain she caused. 'I'll tell him. But I'm sure my father won't print anything.' He knew what would happen if he did!

'Those men work for him, he's responsible for them. And they actually stole those things, took them from my house without permission. You'd better make sure these threats get back to them.'

'I will. I—I'm sorry I brought this trouble on you,

Joel,' she said quietly. 'And I'm sorry for the things I said at the concert hall. I didn't mean them.'

His expression became withdrawn. 'Nevertheless, you said them. Is that really what you think of me?'

'You know it isn't!' There were unshed tears in her eyes. 'Do you forgive me?'

'I'll think about it.'

'And I can bring the things over tomorrow?' she asked eagerly.

'Not tomorrow, I'll be busy. It's the truth,' he said impatiently at her sceptical look. 'I have people to see. I'm arranging for the musical I wrote in Scotland to be staged.'

'I didn't know you'd written a musical,' she gasped.

'Well, you know now. And that's another bit of privileged information I'd rather you didn't tell Daddy or Freed.'

'I wouldn't,' she pouted. 'If I can't see you tomorrow then when can I see you?'

'Aren't you being a little pushy for an engaged woman?' he taunted. 'What would Freed think of you wanting to come to my apartment?'

'I don't care. Joel, I——'

'Not here, Sabina,' he snapped tersely. 'Come to my apartment on Monday. We'll talk about it then.'

She blinked nervously. 'It?'

'The affair you wanted to have with me. I was just going to give in, you know, that day you left Scotland. In fact I thought you'd realised that and that was the reason you suddenly disappeared. But you're still willing, aren't you?' he taunted. his grey eyes insolently appraising her body.

'Joel——'

'Monday.' His hand caressed the bareness of her arm. 'Will you be able to get away?'

She gulped. 'Yes. But——'

'The afternoon then, about two-thirty?' His voice was husky.

'That would be fine. But, Joel, I——'

'Your fiancé is looking this way,' he interrupted softly. 'Smile, Sabina, or he'll think I'm insulting you.'

But he had! She didn't want an *affair* with him, she loved him, and she didn't want that love degraded by having secret meetings with him. But they would have to be secret if they were to meet at all; Nicholas would hardly approve of her seeing him.

She gave an uncertain smile. 'Joel——'

'Your fiancé and his ex-wife don't seem to be getting along too badly, do they?' he remarked thoughtfully. 'And considering Nancy has always professed to hate him I find that rather surprising.'

Sabina looked frowningly at the other couple, smiling as Nicholas looked over at them. They appeared to have stopped arguing now; Nicholas's hand was on Nancy's arm as they seemed to be having a serious conversation.

'Not missing you too badly, is he?' Joel taunted with amusement.

Sabina flushed. 'Nicholas told me that you had an affair with Nancy!' she snapped, stung by his sarcasm.

'Did he now?' He still seemed amused. 'Perhaps he gets a kick out of thinking other men want his women. Maybe that's why he doesn't mind my talking to you now.'

She frowned. 'Are you saying you didn't have an affair with her?'

Joel quirked an eyebrow. 'What do you think?'

'I think you did.' She held her breath as she waited for his answer to her challenge.

To her chagrin he just shrugged it off. 'Then I won't bother to deny it.'

That was no answer! 'Did you?' she persisted.

'Make your own mind up.'

She gave him a long searching look, finally coming to her decision. 'You didn't.'

He smiled. 'You make your mind up suddenly about me, don't you?' The smile faded. 'But when it suits you you change your mind again. As you did tonight about Nicole.'

'Yes. I—I felt guiltier than ever when you sang that song to her.'

'When I——! How the hell do you know it was for her?' he demanded harshly.

Because it had been there in the raw agony of his face. 'Everyone thought so,' she defended. 'She was the girl who went away, wasn't she?'

'Mind your own damned business!' he rasped.

'I'm sorry, I didn't mean to intrude.' Oh dear, she couldn't say anything right where this man was involved.

His mouth twisted mockingly. 'Just be there on Monday, you can intrude as much as you like then.'

'About Monday,' she licked her lips nervously, 'I——'

'You don't want to come?' His gaze was rapier-sharp.

'Yes. I—I want to see Satan.' She blushed in her confusion.

'Only Satan?' he mused.

'Well . . .'

He laughed huskily. 'He'll be pleased to see you, too. I must say I've quite missed my companion from Scotland. Going to bed just isn't the same any more.'

Sabina's cheeks flamed with colour. 'That remark could be misconstrued if anyone overheard it.' She looked about them guiltily.

'No one overheard,' Joel grinned. 'But here comes

your *loving* fiancé, without his ex-wife, I might add. What have you done with Nancy?' he asked Nicholas as he joined them.

Nicholas scowled at him. 'I haven't done anything with her. She went off to talk to one of her damned friends.'

Joel nodded. 'She has a habit of doing that.'

'I know,' Nicholas snapped.

'And now I want to ask you if I can borrow your fiancée for a while.' Joel voiced lightly.

'What?' Nicholas turned to give Sabina a suspicious look, not noticing her suddenly pale face.

What was Joel up to now? Whatever it was she knew Nicholas wasn't going to like it. She wasn't even sure she did.

'I've asked Sabina if she'll help me look for a house,' Joel told him. 'She's very kindly agreed.'

'Sabina?' Nicholas queried sharply.

Oh, lord! What on earth had Joel told Nicholas that for? 'I—I did offer.' Yesterday, not today!

'But you have too much to do,' Nicholas insisted. 'We're getting married in two weeks' time,' he told Joel.

'I know,' he nodded. 'But your fiancée said she had the time to help me out.'

'Sabina?'

Nicholas wanted her to say she had changed her mind, she knew that. And by the challenge in Joel's eyes he was half expecting it too. 'I have the time, Nicholas,' she said calmly. 'Everything for the wedding is arranged, and I don't have a lot to do during the day.'

'But——'

'Do you have any objections, Freed?' Joel asked. 'Because if you do . . .'

'Of course he doesn't,' Sabina cut in hastily before Nicholas could reply. 'I—I would like to, Nicholas,' she added pleadingly.

'When would it be?' Nicholas was obviously still dis-
gruntled, and Sabina couldn't altogether blame him, it
had been rather sprung on him—and her!

'Monday afternoon,' he was calmly informed by Joel.

So that was it! Clever Joel. Now even if she wanted to
refuse, which if she was really honest she didn't, then
Joel had made it impossible for her to do so.

CHAPTER SEVEN

'WHY the hell did you agree to a thing like that?'
Nicholas demanded on the drive back to the apartment
Sabina shared with her father. 'I know you said you
were a fan of his, but did you have to offer to help him
look for a house?'

'I didn't offer!' she flashed.

'He said you did.'

'All right, maybe I did,' she said impatiently. 'But
only after he mentioned he didn't have the time.'

'And I suppose you do?' Nicholas snapped angrily.

'I don't have anything else to do.'

'You said he was too busy himself, but the way he
said it you would be looking together.'

'Just a figure of speech,' she hoped! 'I'll be looking,
and then if I find anything suitable I suppose I'll have
to tell him about it.'

'And how are you supposed to know if it's suitable?'
he scorned. 'You have absolutely no experience of
house-hunting.'

Sabina sighed; she had never seen Nicholas so
agitated. And with just cause, she had to admit. But
even though it displeased her fiancé she knew she had
to see Joel, on Monday or any other time he wanted to
see her. 'You're being ridiculous,' she told Nicholas
now. 'We'll obviously discuss what he wants before I
even approach any agents.'

'A secretary could do that for him—I'm sure he must
have one. Or even the agents themselves could do what
you intend doing.'

She frowned. 'Are you jealous?'

'Don't be stupid!' he exploded. 'I just don't like the man.'

'Why?'

'Why?' He looked irritated. 'Does there have to be a reason?' He stopped the car outside her home, turning in his seat to look at her.

'I think so,' she nodded.

'Well, there isn't one. I just don't like his type. And I would rather you'd talked to me about it before agreeing to help him. I don't——'

'You don't own me, Nicholas,' Sabina told him furiously.

'Sabina——'

'I will not be ordered about by anyone, do you hear?'

He sighed. 'We can't talk here, let's go inside.'

Fortunately her father had gone to bed; food and drink had been left out for them by the maid if they wanted it. Neither of them made a move to touch any of it.

'Now let's get this straight, Nicholas,' Sabina said firmly. 'We may be marrying in two weeks' time, and when that happens I'll owe you a certain loyalty, but I don't expect it to stop me having my friends.'

His look was scornful. 'You think Brent wants to be your *friend*?'

'I think he just wants some help finding a house.' Her cheeks were fiery red. 'That's an innocent enough request, surely?'

Nicholas shook his head. 'I can't say I like it.'

'I'm not asking that you like it, only that you accept it.'

'All right,' he shrugged his shoulders resignedly. 'As long as it doesn't interfere with any of our own plans I won't say another word against it. Just don't get in too deep.'

On the drive over to Joel's apartment on Monday Sabina told herself the same thing. But when you were in love with someone weren't you in as deep as you could go?

Joel answered the door to her himself, taking her through to the lounge. 'Excuse the mess,' he muttered. There were newspapers and other papers all over the room. 'I haven't had time to get a housekeeper yet, either.'

Sabina watched him as he picked up some of the papers to make room for her on the sofa, saw how the faded denims and blue sweat-shirt emphasised the breadth of his shoulders, the narrowness of his waist, and the powerfulness of his muscular thighs.

'That's all right.' She sat down nervously. 'Would you like me to see to that too?'

He quirked an eyebrow, the dark growth of a beard still on his chin, his face pale from lack of sleep. 'Too?' he queried softly.

'As finding you a house.'

'As finding . . .?' He gave a husky laugh. 'Now we both know that isn't the reason you're here.'

'We—we do?' She swallowed hard.

'Of course.' He put up a hand to his chin. 'You'll have to excuse the way I look. I went to a party last night and didn't get back until noon today.'

Sabina's mouth tightened, her imagination instantly going into overdrive, her jealousy like a physical pain. 'I see,' she rasped, looking anywhere but at him. 'Then perhaps you would like to postpone this meeting until a more convenient time.'

'Not on your life!' he grinned.

'Did you have a good time at this party?' Her voice was stilted.

'So prim!' he taunted. 'Yes, it wasn't bad.'

'I—I suppose you've been to a lot of parties since you got back?'

'A few,' he nodded. 'I'd almost forgotten the— pleasures London has to offer.'

Sabina drew a ragged breath. 'You're enjoying being back, then?' she continued this torture.

'It's just as if I'd never been away,' Joel drawled.

And as if their time in Scotland together had never happened! This man wasn't the Joel she had fallen in love with, the man she had come to know during that brief time at the cottage.

'Where's Satan?' she asked, her manner cold.

'In my bedroom. I rigged up a sleeping box for him in there, but he seems to prefer the bed. He hardly ever moves out of there. Come and see him,' he invited, holding out his hand to her.

In his bedroom? She couldn't! She was too vulnerable, too susceptible to the charm he could display when it suited him. 'I—Couldn't you bring him out here?'

His eyes mocked her, his hand falling back to his side. 'I have to make the bed anyway, so you might as well come through and talk to him while I do it.'

The bedroom was in as bad a state as the lounge, with clothes littering the floor, the bed a rumpled mass of blankets and sheets. Curled up in the centre of this mound was Satan. Sabina bent to stroke him. 'Why have you let everywhere get so untidy?' she wanted to know. 'You always kept the cottage so neat.'

Joel shrugged, handing her the cat while he began to tidy the bed. 'I had more time there.'

'No parties,' Sabina said bitterly.

'That's right.' He smiled. 'What did your fiancé have

to say after you left on Saturday?'

'There's no need to sound so amused!' she snapped. 'He wasn't very pleased, naturally.'

'Why naturally? Did you make the same objections about him spending so long with his ex-wife at the party?'

'Don't be silly.' She sighed impatiently, pushing him out of the way. 'For goodness' sake let me do that! You really are hopeless.'

Joel stood back, watching her with undisguised pleasure. 'Maybe I just prefer to see a woman do these things.'

'So I noticed at the cottage.' She put the finishing touches to the bedspread.

'Didn't you think Nicholas and Nancy were just a little too friendly at the party?' He watched her with narrowed eyes.

She had, but she wasn't about to admit it. 'Why shouldn't they be friendly?' she said carelessly. 'Surely after all this time they can be civilised about their divorce?'

'Would you be?'

'I'm not aiming to get divorced. Marriage just needs working at, like everything else in life worth having.'

'Nice idea,' Joel taunted. 'I wonder whether you'll be able to put it into practice, with Freed.'

'There's no reason why I shouldn't.' She couldn't look at him as he lay full-length on the newly made bed, moving to pick up his clothes and put them on the chair.

'There's a very good reason, I would have thought.' He rolled over to lean on his elbow, patting the bed beside him. 'Come and join me.'

Colour flooded her cheeks. 'I came here to discuss houses with you, not to share your bed.'

'But I've missed you, Sabina.' His voice lowered persuasively. 'I don't like sleeping alone.'

'I don't suppose you've done much of that!' she snapped.

'Green eyes again, Sabina?'

'My eyes are always green, and it certainly isn't through jealousy!'

'Isn't it?' he taunted softly. 'Don't you still love me, Sabina?'

She went white, those green eyes he kept taunting her about the only colour in her face. 'That was cruel!' she choked.

'Cruel to remind you of the ploys you were using to get me into bed with you? But I'm trying to tell you that you don't need to use any more ploys. I'm more than willing to go to bed with you right now.'

She shook her head. 'No, Joel . . .' She backed away as he got up from the bed and started to come towards her.

'No?' He quirked an eyebrow mockingly. 'No, perhaps not, not before I've shaved and taken a shower. Would you care to join me in the latter?'

She trembled at the thought of it. 'No! Joel, you're suffering from a misapprehension. I really did come here to help you choose a house. Satan shouldn't be kept here any longer, he needs his freedom, the exercise he can't get here.' She picked the cat up as he slunk around her ankles. 'Look at him, he's starting to look overweight already.'

'You're right,' Joel sighed. 'He isn't happy here. But then neither am I. Come back to Scotland with me, Sabina,' he said suddenly.

'Scotland . . .? But you're arranging your musical.'

'And you're getting married. Let's forget it all and go back to the cottage.'

She was tempted. Oh, how she was tempted! But she

couldn't do it. She had given her word to Nicholas, and it was a promise she couldn't break. 'I'm sorry, that isn't possible,' she told Joel in a stilted voice. 'But I'm more than willing to help you look for a house down here.'

His hand came out to move caressingly down her arm. 'You'll move in with me?'

'No, I—I can't. I'm marrying Nicholas, and I—I'm not the type to indulge in affairs.'

'Aren't you? I thought you were,' he said insultingly.

Sabina swung away from him, opening her handbag and handing him a brown envelope that contained his possessions. 'Here,' she thrust them at him when he made no move to take it. She put them down on the dressing-table. 'Now we have no further reason to meet. Goodbye, Joel.'

'Oh no, you don't!' He grabbed her arm. 'We have a very good reason to meet, you want me and I want you. And until you're ready to come to me willingly I'll keep up this pretence of looking for a house. You'll find a list of agents next to the telephone in the lounge. Give some of them a call while I get tidied up,' he said briskly.

She drew an angry breath. 'So you do intend buying a house!' she accused. 'How dare you play that game with me? How——'

'No game, Sabina,' he interrupted darkly. 'I want you and I mean to get you. But I've never used force on a woman and I don't intend making you a first. Anyway,' his voice lightened, 'I've noticed the weight Satan's put on too. He needs a few dozen mice to chase, that should get the fat off him.'

'Maybe you just shouldn't feed him so much,' she said pertly.

'I seem to remember that you were always the one who sneaked him half the food off your own plate,' he reminded her teasingly.

Sabina blushed. 'Well, he always looked at me so soulfully.'

Joel's eyes darkened almost to black. 'And if I look at you like that will you give me a few tasty morsels?' he asked throatily.

'I'll go and make those calls!' She hurriedly made her escape.

As it turned out she had to sit and wait for Joel to make an appearance. She had forgotten to ask him what sort of house he wanted, how many rooms, any land attached, in the country or here in London. The wait gave her plenty of time to think of Joel and the proposition he had just made to her.

If it weren't for the promise she had given Nicholas, would she have gone back to Scotland with Joel? Without hesitation came the immediate answer. So much for her assertion that she didn't have affairs!

Joel came into the room and noticed her frown. 'Changed your mind?' he grinned.

'No. And I shall leave right now if you're going to bring that into every conversation.'

'I'm not,' he smiled. 'Have any luck?' he indicated the list.

'You didn't tell me what you're looking for.' She wished she could take her eyes off him; her hungry gaze locked on how attractive he looked in slate grey trousers and a lighter grey fitted shirt, her senses alive to how totally male he was. 'What your requirements are,' she added by way of explanation.

His expression was wickedly teasing. '*You're* my requirement, Sabina, every delicious inch of you.'

'Joel!'

'Okay, okay.' He sat down in the chair opposite her. 'I see you tidied up.' He looked about the now neat room.

'Not as much as I'd like to.' It irritated her beyond words how he could change from being verbally seductive to practical in the space of a few seconds!

He opened his arms wide, leaning back in the chair. 'Feel free.'

'Get yourself a housekeeper!'

'It isn't worth it, not when I expect to be moving soon.'

'Maybe not,' Sabina accepted. 'I'll finish the cleaning in a minute. Now what sort of house did you have in mind?'

He pursed his lips thoughtfully. 'What do you think?'

'Well, I don't know, do I?' she dismissed shortly. 'I don't know what you like.'

'I could soon teach you,' he said huskily.

'Let's get this straight now,' Sabina snapped. 'Either we go into this seriously or we forget the whole thing. I'm not here for your amusement.'

Joel shrugged. 'I want something not too big, but not too small either. Somewhere I can feel at home. A family home, I suppose I mean.'

Sabina's eyes widened with shock, her breath seeming to catch in her throat. 'You're thinking of getting married?'

'Don't you know it's natural to want to procreate the race?' he taunted.

Colour flamed her cheeks. 'But Nicole . . .'

His face instantly became a shuttered mask. 'Is part of the past,' he finished harshly. 'And I want a future.'

'Then why write songs about her?' she choked. 'Why stand on a stage and pour your heart out to her, so that not one person watching you can mistake the love you still have for her?'

' "The Girl Who Went Away",' he said softly.

'That's right,' Sabina was becoming very upset now. 'Why don't you let her die!'

'She is dead!' He stood forcibly to his feet, glaring down at her with flinty eyes. 'A once beautiful girl grown ugly and obscene, no longer beautiful in her pain. She is dead, Sabina. Dead, dead, *dead*!' His voice had risen to a shout.

Her breath caught in a sob. 'Then let her go, Joel. *Let her go!*'

'And replace her with someone like you?' he scorned. 'Someone who ran scared at the sudden realisation of her marriage being only weeks away? Someone who was willing to go to bed with me, with any man, because you suddenly felt trapped, who even now can't stay away from me? Don't bother to deny it, Sabina,' he rasped as she went to speak. 'You almost begged me to let you come here. And now you are here you're running scared again. I wonder if Freed will be able to catch you on your wedding night.'

'You're cruel and barbarous!' she choked. 'And you like to hurt.'

'Women like you have made me the way I am. Why is it some women like to be hurt, to be degraded?' His fingers dug into her arms as he shook her. 'Well, if you want to grovel, Sabina, you just go right ahead. Right now I'd make love to you no matter what you did.' He pushed her down on the couch, swiftly following her, his weight pinning her down. 'Go ahead and fight me, Sabina, and we'll see how long that lasts.'

His lips ground down on hers, the salty taste in her mouth and the stinging on the inside of her lip telling her that he had actually split the inside of her mouth with the savagery of his assault. But he seemed to care nothing for her pain, forcing her to accept his kisses, his hands on her body. And Sabina felt as if she were dying, her emotions numb.

'You've stopped fighting,' Joel taunted triumphantly. 'You're just like all the rest, Sabina. The more men hurt you and take you for granted the more eager you are.' He stood up, going over to the window and staring out, his back rigid. When he finally turned back Sabina had swung her feet to the ground and was smoothing back her tousled blonde hair. 'I thought you were different,' he said harshly, accusingly.

'I am.' Her eyes were huge pools of humiliation. 'If you think I enjoyed that attack then you're mistaken. I don't know what sort of women you've known in the past,' her voice broke, the tears started to fall, 'but I didn't like that—that insult!'

'So you want to be loved, hmm?' His words were bitter. 'Well, I'm sorry, Miss Smith, but I'm not in the mood.'

'And I'm not in the mood to put up with your insults!' She stood angrily to her feet. 'Barbarian is too mild a word for you, you—you *animal*, you!' She swung past him on her way to the door.

'Sabina . . .' Miraculously his mood had changed once again, his voice soft and enticing. He pulled her up against him. 'I'm sorry,' he said huskily. 'Will you forgive me?'

Her eyes flashed. 'You think you just have to utter a few words of apology and it wipes out that—that attack you just made on me? Well, let me tell you——' her words were cut off by the placing of his lips on hers. 'Joel——' she tried to wrench away from him.

'I'm sorry,' he repeated softly, a hand either side of her face as he again bent his head to kiss her. 'I'm sorry, Sabina. Sorry . . . Sorry . . . Sorry . . .'

This time his kisses were meant to be enjoyed, his hands running caressingly down her body from breast to thigh. She kissed him back, her mouth opening to the caress of his tongue, her arms going up about his throat to touch the hair at his nape.

His hands were loosely linked at the base of her spine as he gently kissed her brow. 'Am I forgiven? I know my temper's foul, but I've asked you not to talk about Nicole. I try not to even think about her, let alone talk about her.'

'Then why——'

'No questions.' He put his fingers over her lips to silence her. 'No questions and I won't lose my temper again.' He put her away from him. 'Shall we see about those houses now?'

'You mean you still want my help?' Sabina was still dazed by his kisses.

'I would value a woman's opinion.'

She looked away. 'I didn't realise you were getting married. Do I know your intended bride?' What a strange question to be asking the man who had just kissed her so passionately. But no stranger than her being engaged and yet still *letting* him kiss her!

'I didn't say anything about getting married,' Joel mocked her.

Colour flooded her cheeks. 'Oh! You mean . . . I see,' she bit her bottom lip.

'A lot of people don't bother with the legalities any more. Come on, let's get that phoning done.'

'I thought you were too busy.'

'By the look of Satan I'll have to make time for this. He can't stay here much longer.'

For the next hour they telephoned the agencies Joel had on his list, finally coming up with three houses that sounded promising. Joel made appointments to view one at five o'clock today, and the other two the next day.

'That's okay with you, isn't it?' he asked on the

drive to the first house.

Sabina looked startled. 'You want me to come with you tomorrow too?'

He shrugged. 'If this one doesn't turn out to be what I want.'

' "Situated by the Thames, set in two acres of land",' Sabina read the details he had written down. ' "Eight bedrooms". Will you really want that many?' She looked at him.

'Depends on how many children we have.'

'Children . . .?' she echoed.

'Mm. Of course I'll have to marry when they start to come along.'

Sabina was very pale. 'When do I get to meet the woman in your life?'

'Oh, you've already met her. Deeside Drive,' he read the sign. 'Isn't there something like that in the directions?'

She hastily looked down at the list of instructions. 'Yes, here it is. We turn right here. I've already met her, you said?' she persisted.

'Her? Joel frowned, his concentration on his driving. 'Oh yes, yes, you have.'

'When——'

'Holly Grove,' he read. 'Is that on the list, Sabina?'

'Er—oh yes. Yes, turn left here.'

'I nearly missed that,' he said tersely. 'For heaven's sake concentrate on the directions. We told the estate agent we would be there at five, it's past that now. If you concentrate more on those instructions and less on my personal affairs we might manage to get there before five-thirty.'

'Yes, sir!' Sabina slanted him a look of resentment.

For the rest of the drive she rapped out instructions, her abrupt behaviour seeming to amuse Joel. As he had predicted, it was almost five-thirty by the time they reached the house, and the agent instantly got out of his car to come over to them.

Joel had already greeted the man before Sabina had had time to get out of the Porsche and join them. The agent had obviously realised that Mr Brent was *the* Joel Brent, and was fawning all over him, his manner making Sabina cringe.

'Sabina Smith, Bill Symons,' Joel introduced curtly.

'Miss Smith,' the agent gushed. 'I'll show you and your fiancée round now, shall I?' he asked Joel.

'Oh, but——'

'Fine,' Joel agreed smoothly, cutting in on Sabina's protest. 'The grounds seem suitable, anyway.'

'Very nice for a young family.' Bill Symons walked with them to the house. 'The fence covers the whole of the perimeter, making for complete privacy.'

Sabina glared at Joel as he grinned down at her, obviously enjoying the man's enthusiastic sales talk. She shut herself off as they toured the house, imagining that she really was Joel's fiancée, and that they really would be sharing this house. How she wished it were true!

The lounge ran from one end of the house to the other, another reception room off this, a study, the kitchen, although Joel mockingly assured her that would be 'her' province, fitted with every modern convenience going. Sabina thought longingly of the tiny kitchen they had shared in Scotland, caring nothing for the modern conveniences if she could just be back there with Joel.

The upstairs was lovely too. Besides the eight spacious bedrooms there were four luxury bathrooms, one of them connected to the master bedroom.

'And this door,' Bill Symons opened a door connected the opposite side, 'leads to a nursery.' He looked at Sabina's slender figure. 'Of course, you won't be needing that for a while,' he joked. 'But it pays to plan ahead when buying a house.'

'It does indeed.' Joel's eyes taunted Sabina as her colour flooded her cheeks. 'There you are, darling,' he put an arm about her shoulders. 'You can put your mind at rest about having the baby close to you at night.'

'Yes,' she replied through gritted teeth.

'Shall we look at the other bedrooms?' Joel spoke briskly to the agent.

'Of course,' he nodded. 'If you'll just come this way I'll show them to you.' He went on ahead.

'You louse!' Sabina stormed at Joel. 'How dare you let him think we're going to be married?'

He shrugged, completely relaxed—and enjoying himself immensely at her expense. 'The truth would be even harder to understand. Even I'm not sure what you want to be in my life. One minute you can't wait to be alone with me, and the next you're running away.'

'And I'm going to keep on running,' she told him in a fierce whisper as they almost caught up with the agent. 'And one more crack about my being your wife and I'm likely to hit you!'

'And shock Mr Symons?' he taunted.

'Yes!'

'Promises, promises,' he mocked.

'I'll make it reality in a minute,' she threatened.

'Try it and see,' he encouraged, openly laughing at her now.

'I hate you!'

'Strange you keep coming back,' he taunted. 'Yes, Mr Symons,' he said in a bored voice as the agent tried to regain his attention and show him the rest of the top floor. 'Very nice.'

'Ideal for guests,' the man started to babble as he realised he was losing his client's interest. 'I presume you entertain quite a lot. The previous owner——'

'Not a lot,' Joel told him. 'I prefer my privacy.'

'Oh well,' the man changed his tactics, 'there's plenty of room for that too.'

'Perhaps too much room. We'd get lost in a place like this,' Joel half smiled. 'It would take me hours to find my wife,' his arm went about Sabina's waist, 'and you have to admit, when I wanted her I'd want her in a hurry.'

A dark hue coloured the agent's fleshy cheeks. 'Yes, well . . .'

'I'd make sure you found me, darling,' Sabina murmured huskily, the sparkle in her eyes shooting out darts of dislike at him. 'Or I'd find you,' she added almost threateningly.

'I'm sure you would,' he laughed meaningly. 'The decor is lousy too, Mr Symons,' he indicated the floral wallpaper in the hallway. 'It would take weeks to decorate it the way I would want it. Whoever chose this stuff had terrible taste.'

'The previous owner was one of those terrible pop stars——' once again colour flooded his cheeks. 'I mean—Oh dear . . . I didn't mean—Mr Brent, I——'

Joel was having trouble holding back the laughter, Sabina could clearly see that. 'Forget it, Mr Symons,' he drawled. 'I don't consider myself a pop star.'

'Of course not, Mr Brent,' but the poor man obviously considered he had lost ground on this sale. 'I haven't shown you the most attractive feature yet, something I'm sure you'll be interested in Mr Brent.'

'Oh yes?' Joel didn't look impressed.

'Yes.' The agent looked quietly confident.

Sabina walked down the stairs beside Joel, having difficulty in containing her own amusement. That Bill Symons, a man in his mid-fifties, considered Joel to be one of those 'terrible pop stars' she found highly amusing.

They went out of the front door, round the side of the house to the stables. But it wasn't the stables themself that he seemed intent on showing them, it was the room over the top of them. And Sabina soon realised why. It was a recording room, all the equipment still in working order, the walls and floor soundproof.

Joel walked slowly around the room, touching things, his pleasure evident. But he said nothing, not then, and not during their leavetaking a few minutes later. Bill Symons seemed disappointed by his lack of enthusiasm, obviously expecting more reaction to his little surprise. Joel's silence on the subject also surprised Sabina; she had thought the recording room was sure to make him buy.

'I'll let you know,' he told the agent haughtily.

'But, Mr Brent——'

'Thank you for giving us your time,' Joel told him carelessly, as he swung into the car beside Sabina. 'But we have other houses to look at before making any final decision.'

'Didn't you like it?' Sabina asked curiously once they were on their way back to town.

He shrugged. 'It seemed okay to me, but then I have nothing to compare it with, do I?' His expression lightened. 'Did you see his face when he thought I'd taken offence over being called a pop star?' He gave a throaty chuckle.

Sabina started to laugh too. 'The poor man was devastated,' she laughed.

Joel's expression deepened to intimacy as he looked at her. 'Have dinner with me tonight?'

She blushed at that look. 'I—I can't. I'm meeting Nicholas.' When he would no doubt grill her about this meeting with Joel!

His face darkened with displeasure. 'Break it,' he ordered abruptly.

Her eyes sparkled rebelliously. 'I will not! I happen to be marrying him.'

'Break that too. You don't love him.'

'Mind your own business!'

'Okay, I will!' His foot pressed down hard on the accelerator, the Porsche eating up the miles. 'When you want it to be my business again let me know.'

'I never made it your business in the first place,' she told him furiously. 'No one asked you to keep making love to me.'

'No one asked me to stop either,' he snapped.

'Well, I'm asking now. Just leave me alone.'

His expression was grim. 'You promised to help me look for a house, and you'll do just that.'

'I didn't promise!' Sabina made a point of never promising anything to anyone now, not when it was her promises to Nicholas and her father that were trapping her into a marriage she didn't want.

'Okay, so you didn't *promise*, but you did offer, and I accepted. So I'll pick you up at ten o'clock tomorrow. Right?' he said forcefully.

'Right,' she echoed hollowly. She was willing to accept any crumb, her relief was so immense at him not accepting the first house they had looked at. At least this way she had a valid excuse for seeing him again.

CHAPTER EIGHT

NICHOLAS was strangely uncommunicative that evening, listening to Sabina halfheartedly as she told him about the house she and Joel had viewed.

'So you liked it,' he said uninterestedly.

'Yes,' she frowned. 'Although Joel didn't seem too keen.'

'I thought he wouldn't be with you?' he asked sharply.

'He had a free afternoon.' She couldn't meet his eyes.

'I see. If he didn't like the house then perhaps we should buy it.' He lit up a cigar after their meal in one of London's leading restaurants, where the quiet, efficient service was to his liking.

'I thought you didn't want a house.'

He shrugged, leaning back in his chair and waving the waiter away as he brought them more coffee. 'If you liked it . . .'

He was prepared to be indulgent, Sabina could see that. She also knew that by morning he would have changed his mind, that he probably wouldn't even remember this conversation, that he wasn't even listening to her. Wherever his mind was it wasn't with her, he seemed to drift off every time she spoke to him. And she was glad! She didn't want to share a house with him that she had imagined living in with Joel.

'I didn't like it that much,' she lied. She had loved the house, had wanted to live there with Joel, could imagine a baby with his dark hair and grey eyes in the nursery—her baby.

'Nicholas . . .' She bit her lip. 'Nicholas, how do you

feel about children?'

That brought him out of his reverie. 'Children?' he repeated sharply. 'You mean ours?'

She blushed at his air of surprise. 'Well, of course, ours. We *are* going to be married.'

'I know that,' he said impatiently. 'But we've never discussed the possibility of having children.'

'Exactly! Do you want them?'

'In time,' he answered evasively. 'Yes, I suppose so.'

'In time?' Her eyes widened. 'But you're forty-five now!'

'And you're nineteen, much too young to be a mother.'

'So you don't want children,' Sabina said dully.

'I didn't say that, I said in time.'

'And we'll have a nanny, of course.'

'Of course,' he agreed readily, her sarcasm lost on him. 'You won't have to be bothered with things like bringing up children.'

'And if I want to be bothered?'

He laughed at her fierce expression. 'What is this, Sabina? Are you trying to pick an argument with me?'

'I simply wanted to discuss whether or not we're going to have a family. I consider that a perfectly normal conversation for an engaged couple.'

'Maybe it is,' Nicholas snapped. 'But I'm not in the mood to discuss it this evening. And I hardly think this is the right place. We were talking about that house you viewed today,' he reminded her.

'I'd rather live in your apartment,' she told him in a stilted voice.

'So would I,' he said with obvious relief.

'I—er—I agreed to go and look at two more houses with Joel tomorrow.' She looked at him nervously.

'Why on earth did you do that?' He sounded angry.

'You've fulfilled your obligation, why continue to see him?'

'Well, he——'

'Do you *want* to see him?' Nicholas's eyes were narrowed suspiciously.

'Of course not. I just——'

'I think you do, Sabina,' he rasped. 'Are you attracted to him?' he demanded.

'No! He—he's getting married himself soon,' she said desperately, anxious to convince him.

Nicholas frowned. 'He is? But who——' his gaze passed beyond Sabina and he seemed to pale. 'Speak of the devil!' he muttered.

'What——?' Sabina turned in time to see Joel and Nancy Freed just leaving one of the completely private cubicles farther up the restaurant. Joel and *Nancy*! Oh no, it couldn't be her he was marrying, could it? But why not? Nicholas said they had been more than friendly in the past, Joel hadn't denied it, and they had been at that party together on Saturday. Yes, it had to be Nancy Freed he intended sharing a house with and eventually marrying.

Nicholas scowled as the other couple made their way towards the exit. They would have to pass their table, so Nicholas's displeasure was understandable.

Nancy Freed saw them first, and her smile deepened as she stopped next to their table. 'Fancy seeing you two here!' Her exclamation of pleasure seemed genuine.

'Fancy,' Joel drawled at her side, looking Sabina up and down with barely concealed insolence.

She was instantly made aware of how low-cut the neckline was of the dress she was wearing, the tan colour emphasising the blondeness of her hair and the golden glow of her skin. Joel missed none of this, and a taunting light entered his eyes as the dark colour washed over her cheeks.

'Brent,' Nicholas nodded his greeting distantly.

'Have you finished your meal?' Nancy asked him eagerly.

'Why, yes. But——'

'Then come to the club with us,' his ex-wife invited with enthusiasm. 'Joel and I were just going to Scenes.' She put her hand in the crook of her escort's arm. 'Wouldn't it be nice if Sabina and Nicholas came with us?'

Joel seemed to consider her beautiful upturned face for several long minutes. 'Yes,' he answered slowly. 'Yes, I think it just might be.'

And Sabina thought the opposite! If she had to spend too long in their company she might betray her true feelings, and that would never do. She turned to Nicholas. 'I'm really not in the mood for music and dancing tonight.' Her voice was almost pleading.

Sharp blue eyes were turned on her, the smile on Nancy Freed's lips not reaching those deep blue orbs. 'As you're the youngest one here I would have thought you would have liked all that the club has to offer.'

'She isn't that young,' Nicholas snapped resentfully.

'Isn't she?' his ex-wife queried softly. 'Well, perhaps not. But I'm sure you'll enjoy yourself, Sabina. I've always found I enjoy something more if I haven't been looking forward to it. Oh, do come, you two,' she encouraged impatiently.

'Sabina?' Nicholas was obviously weakening.

She sighed her reluctance, looking up to meet taunting grey eyes. Joel knew she was refusing because of him—and he found it amusing! Her mouth set rebelliously. 'Yes, I think I would like to go after all.'

'Oh, good,' Nancy smiled. 'Did you bring your car, Nicholas? We didn't bother as we both live so close.'

'Oh, I see.' Nicholas stood up, scowling heavily. 'I'm to be used as a damned taxi service, am I?'

Nancy's eyes sparkled angrily. 'Don't be so ridiculous! If you feel that way we can easily meet up with you later. I just thought——'

'Now, now, children,' Joel broke up the argument with lazy humour. 'If you have to bicker like the married couple you were, at least wait until we get outside.'

Nancy grimaced. 'Don't remind me!'

'I didn't think you needed reminding,' he drawled softly. Suddenly he turned to looked at Sabina, catching her unawares. 'Are you going to sit there all night?' he taunted.

Colour flamed in her cheeks and she stood up, aware of his appraisal as he noticed how her silky dress moulded to the curves of her body. 'I'm ready to leave if everyone else is,' she said tautly, trembling under that warm appraisal.

She was quiet on the drive to the club, not even listening to the light conversation of her companions. She was too much aware of Joel sitting directly behind her to be able to even think straight, let alone indulge in conversation.

Joel was going to marry Nancy Freed, that was all that seemed important to her. She wondered, rather hysterically, when the wedding would be. Not until there was a child, Joel had said. Did that mean they intended trying to have a baby straight away?

Joel stood beside her in the club, his expression mocking. 'Drink?'

They had arrived a few minutes earlier, and now they were moving to one of the booths. Scenes was exactly what it sounded like, the club a series of rooms showing different scenes from great films. They were in the room from a set of *Gone With the Wind*. But the music was strictly nineteen-eighties, loud pop music that almost blasted the eardrums.

'Sabina?' Joel snapped sharply.

'Yes, I—I'll have an orange juice.' Her eyes flashed her irritation. 'Please.'

His mouth quirked mockingly. 'Tristram doesn't serve anything so innocuous.'

'Tristram?'

'He runs the club.'

'Oh, I see. Well, a Martini, then, with lemonade,' she compromised.

'With lemonade,' Joel taunted.

He disappeared into the crowd and Sabina was left with Nicholas and Nancy, a Nicholas and Nancy who seemed to have stopped arguing and were now just glaring at each other. It was strange that Sabina was the one who felt left out.

Joel came back with the drinks, and sat down next to Sabina, his lean length near enough for her to just reach out and touch. If she had wanted to—which she didn't, couldn't. 'One Martini—with lemonade,' he put the drink down on the table, his grey eyes mocking her.

'Cheers.' Nicholas downed his double whisky in one gulp. 'Anyone else care for another?' He stood up.

They all declined and he went off alone. Sabina was surprised by his actions, he didn't usually drink to excess, and they had already had a bottle of wine with their meal earlier.

'I wonder what's eating him,' Joel mused.

'I wonder,' Nancy echoed thoughtfully. She too stood up. 'I'll be back in a minute, darling,' she ran her hand caressingly down Joel's cheek. 'I've just seen someone I want to talk to.'

He gave her a lazy smile. 'Don't worry about us. I'm sure Sabina will keep me amused.'

Nancy's eyes widened. 'Really?' She looked at Sabina. 'She doesn't look in the mood to amuse anyone right now.'

Sabina glared at Joel once the other woman had walked off in the direction of the bar. 'I'm sick of amusing you,' she told him angrily. 'All you ever do is laugh at me.'

'What's the matter?' he drawled. 'Don't you love me any more?'

'Ooh!' Her mouth set mutinously. 'Why are you always so cruel to me?' To her shame her voice broke emotionally. 'Just because I was once stupid enough to tell you I'm in love with you it doesn't mean you have to keep throwing it up in my face every time we meet!'

'So you don't love me?'

Colour flooded her face. 'No, I don't!' she said indignantly.

Joel gave a husky laugh. 'Then you'll be quite happy to marry Nicholas next week, won't you?'

Sabina stood up, her green eyes deepened with pain. 'God, I hate you! I—I——' her voice trembled and tears welled up in her eyes. 'Oh, Joel,' she groaned before turning away and making her way blindly through the groups of chattering people.

A hand clamped about her upper arm and she was pulled in the direction of the dance space, feeling herself pulled into firm muscular arms as she blinked back the tears.

'Nicholas——'

The arms tightened painfully about her waist. 'Never again mistake me for Freed,' Joel growled.

Sabina raised a startled face, blushing as she realised how close she was dancing to him, his hands linked loosely at the bass of her spine. 'Joel . . .' she said breathlessly.

His head swooped and his lips caressed her throat. 'Never doubt it,' he murmured huskily.

'Joel—please!' she squirmed against him. 'Joel, Nicholas might see us!' She looked about them guiltily, expecting at any moment to see Nicholas's furious face in the crowd.

'Let him,' he dismissed carelessly.

'But Nancy might see us too,' she said desperately.

He raised his head. 'So?'

'So you're going to marry her,' Sabina snapped. 'I don't think she would appreciate you holding me like this.'

Joel's eyes narrowed. 'Would it surprise you to know I couldn't give a damn?'

It didn't surprise her at all. Joel was a man who lived by his own rules, regardless of anyone else's feelings. 'Joel, please!' she repeated worriedly as his lips moved against her earlobe, sending ripples of pleasure through her body. 'Stop it,' she pleaded. 'People are looking at us.'

'Rubbish,' he dismissed huskily. 'Everyone else is doing the same thing.'

They were too, some of the couples touching more intimately than she and Joel, much to her embarrassment. 'But——'

'Just enjoy it, Sabina—as I am.'

She wanted to, oh, how she wanted to! She relaxed against him, her arms going up about his throat, the dark hair at his nape feeling soft and silky to her touch.

'That's better,' he said with satisfaction, placing featherlight kisses along the line of her jaw. 'You're a delicious bundle of femininity,' he murmured throatily. 'And certainly not to be wasted on Freed.'

Nicholas! She had forgotten him the last few minutes. She pushed away from Joel now as she remembered her

fiancé. 'I think we should go back to the table now.'
She tried to sound distant, but she knew by the derision
in Joel's eyes that she had failed to convince him.

'You know you don't want to,' he taunted softly. 'Just
relax, forget about them.'

'Forget them . . .!' she gasped. 'We can't forget them,
we're going to marry them.'

'You don't want to marry Freed——'

'But you want to marry Nancy!'

He was watching her closely. 'Do I?'

'You told me you did,' she reminded him. 'I want to
go back to the table,' she insisted.

Joel shrugged resignedly, his arms dropping to his
sides. 'So be it.'

Sabina led the way back, aware of her disappointment
at him accepting her decision. What had she expected
him to do, sweep her off her feet and carry her off to—
to where? To Scotland! He had asked her to go back
there with him once today, she didn't think he would
repeat the offer. And she couldn't accept even if he did.

Conversation stopped as they rejoined the other
couple, and Nancy finally forced a smile. 'Where have
you two been?' Her voice was jerky, her hand trembling
slightly as she carried her glass to her mouth.

'Dancing,' Sabina told her shyly, glancing apprehensively at Nicholas. He was scowling at everyone,
another drink on the table in front of him.

'Isn't this nice?' Nancy sat back with a strained smile.

'Lovely,' Joel agreed mockingly.

'And aren't you the lucky one, Nicholas?' Nancy gave
him a look of innocence.

His scowl deepened. 'How do you work that out?' he
rasped harshly.

'Well, there can't be many men here tonight who have
two women sitting with them both wearing his ring.'

'What the hell——!'

'But we are, darling,' Nancy said teasingly, holding out her left hand and showing him the gold wedding ring on her third finger. 'See?'

'Why the hell are you still wearing that?' Nicholas growled his displeasure.

'It hasn't been off my finger since the day you put it there,' she told him huskily.

Nicholas flushed, glancing with irritation at Sabina. 'Believe me, she never used to be this romantic,' he taunted.

'And I'm still not,' Nancy flashed. 'But you put it there, you should be the one to take it off.'

'The day I divorced you I was *telling* you to take it off,' he snapped.

He had divorced Nancy? That came as something of a shock to Sabina. Although she found the subject of the conversation rather embarrassing. She was finding the whole evening embarrassing, if the truth were known; her senses were still reeling from being in Joel's arms minutes earlier. This was such an explosive situation—a divorced husband and wife each with other partners, especially as these partners weren't exactly averse to each other.

Nancy held out her left hand to Nicholas. 'Take it off now,' she invited softly. 'Go on, Nick, take it off.'

'Don't call me Nick,' he ordered with repressed violence.

'You once told me I could be the one person that did.'

'I once told you a lot of things!'

'Take the ring off, Nicholas,' she repeated quietly.

'Not here, Nancy.' He was beginning to look uncomfortable now. 'Stop making a scene.'

'Here!' She ripped the ring off her finger, putting it

down on the table before standing up. 'Excuse me,' she said brightly, too brightly, and turned on her heel and hurried off.

Nicholas half rose in his chair, looking down at the gold ring. 'Why the hell did she do that?' he muttered angrily.

'Don't be a fool, Freed,' Joel said impatiently, standing up to follow Nancy.

Sabina stood up too. 'Let me, Joel,' she stopped him.

The look he gave her was derisive. 'I would think you're the last person she wants to see right now.'

She blushed under his censure, her head going back proudly. 'You may be a lot of things, Joel, be able to do a lot of things, but I don't think even you could walk into a ladies' loo and get away with it, because that's where Nancy went. Well?'

The harshness left his face and he gave a shrug of defeat. 'She's all yours.' He sat down again.

It didn't take Sabina long to locate Nancy Freed. She was sitting in front of the mirrors in the powder-room, a freshly lit cigarette between her shaking fingers.

Her eyes widened as she caught sight of Sabina, but she managed to maintain a cool façade. 'Take a pew,' she invited.

Sabina sat on the stool next to her. 'I'm sure Nicholas didn't mean to be cruel,' she said gently. 'He just didn't think.'

Nancy gave a bitter laugh. 'Nick always thinks. I'm not fooled by that charming exterior, I never was. He's as hard as iron, with a mind like a computer. He plays everything to his advantage.'

'Maybe,' Sabina accepted. 'But I think he regrets what he just said and did to you.'

'He never regrets anything either.' Nancy gave a sharp laugh, stubbing out her half-smoked cigarette, and then instantly lighting another one. 'He knew damn well he was humiliating me.'

'I don't think——'

'He knew, damn it!' Nancy stood up to pace the room, uncaring of the other women entering and leaving.

'Not this time,' Sabina disagreed, sure that Nicholas's behaviour had been unpremeditated. He was too drunk to know what he was doing. 'I'm sure he didn't mean to hurt you,' she told Nancy.

Blue eyes flashed anger. 'What makes you think I'm hurt?' Nancy snapped.

'Aren't you?'

Nancy drew a ragged breath. 'Yes, God, *yes*!'

'Because you still love him?'

Nancy came back to sit on the stool. 'I've never stopped loving him,' she admitted dully.

'Even though he used to hit you?'

'Hit me?' She frowned her puzzlement. 'He never— Oh yes, he hit me, once. But I deserved it.'

Sabina shook her head dazedly. As far as she knew Nicholas was a wife-beater. Nancy gave a different impression. 'I don't understand . . .'

Nancy sighed. 'I don't suppose you do. I was a silly little bitch when Nick married me, a very naïve eighteen. I thought Nick was the most wonderful man in the world, wanted him to be equally smitten with me. At thirty-one he was already cynical and worldly, with a five-year marriage behind him. Elly died, you know.'

Sabina did know, her father had told her some time ago. Unusual as it was in this age of medical wonder, Elly Freed had died as the result of a miscarriage.

'Nick loved her very much,' Nancy added with remembered pain.

'But he married you,' Sabina pointed out gently.

'And treated me like a child, to be pampered and

patted on the head when he had the time to notice me. Not surprisingly I rebelled.'

'How?'

Nancy shrugged. 'I told him I was having affairs, that other men wanted me even if he didn't.'

'Was Joel one of these men?' Sabina found herself holding her breath as she waited for her answer.

Nancy smiled. 'Yes.'

'And did you?'

'Have an affair with him?' The other woman laughed as Sabina nodded. 'No. Joel doesn't go in for affairs with married women.'

'But you have him now,' Sabina said bitterly.

'I'm with him, I wouldn't say I have him. After Nicole I don't think any woman will ever get his trust again.'

Sabina's look sharpened. 'You knew Nicole Dupont?'

'Yes, I knew her. She was a vicious-tongued little tramp.'

Sabina wasn't sure whether these were the remarks of a jealous woman, and without showing her own interest in Joel she couldn't ask any further. 'Why did you tell Nick—Nicholas, you were having an affair with Joel if you weren't?'

Nancy sighed. 'I was trying to make him jealous. But all it did was make him angry. That was when he hit me.'

'But you told Joel—Never mind.' Sabina looked away, her face red with embarrassment. 'It doesn't matter. It's none of my business anyway.'

'Did Joel tell you Nick hit me?'

'He—well, he—Yes,' Sabina admitted reluctantly.

'Why?' Nancy asked slowly. 'I mean why did he tell you?'

She shrugged. 'I don't know. Perhaps he thought I ought to know Nicholas is a wife-beater.'

'I see. Mm, interesting. Right,' Nancy smoothed her dress down over her thighs, 'I'm ready to go back to the table now.'

'You're sure you're all right?'

'Yes, fine,' Nancy gave a bright smile. 'I'm glad we had this little chat, Sabina. I like you.'

Strangely enough Sabina liked her too. Underneath the brittle butterfly exterior Nancy Freed was a warm friendly woman who was still very much in love with her ex-husband.

The two men were sitting in armed silence when they rejoined them, Nicholas looking searchingly at Nancy.

'Don't look so apprehensive,' she taunted him. 'I haven't been telling your little bride-to-be all your dark secrets.'

'Then maybe you ought to have done,' Joel drawled.

'What's that supposed to mean?' Nicholas looked as if he had downed a couple of more drinks in their absence, a permanent flush to his cheeks, his eyes slightly fevered.

'What do you think I mean?' Joel challenged.

'I have no idea. Just who do you think——'

'Calm down, Nicholas,' Sabina said quietly.

He turned venomous blue eyes on her. 'Don't tell me what to do!' he snapped.

She took a deep breath in an effort to hold on to her own temper. 'You're causing a scene,' she told him softly.

'I'll cause a scene if I damn well want to,' he said angrily, his tone vicious.

'But——'

'Just shut up and leave me alone, Sabina.' He threw the last of his whisky to the back of his throat, swallowing hard. 'What do you know about anything anyway? You're too damned young,' he muttered almost to himself. 'Too young,' he glowered at her.

She bit her lip. 'Nicholas——'

'Just shut up!'

Joel suddenly sat forward, an air of menace about him. 'If you talk to her like that one more time, Freed, I'm going to hit you,' he told the other man in a soft, dangerous tone.

Nicholas looked startled. 'What did you say?'

'You heard me,' Joel met his gaze unflinchingly. 'Just one more rude comment to Sabina and I'm going to put you at her feet where you belong.'

Nicholas half rose in his chair. 'Why, you——'

Nancy put a hand on his arm. 'Not here, Nick. Please!' Her voice held a wealth of meaning.

He glowered at Joel and sank back into his seat. 'He has no right to talk to me like that. Sabina is *my* fiancée,' he added resentfully.

'I'm still trying to work out why,' Joel drawled insultingly.

'What's that remark supposed to mean?' Nicholas's anger increased.

Joel looked away dismissively. 'Work it out for yourself.'

'No, you tell me. And while you're about it you can tell me what interest you have in my fiancée.'

Grey eyes narrowed threateningly. 'Go to hell, Freed! For some reason Sabina seems loath to upset you, but I don't feel the same reluctance. I think you're an obnoxious little creep. I always have done.'

'Joel!' Sabina gasped. 'Please——'

'Keep out of this,' Nicholas growled.

'Right, that's *it*!' Joel stood up to tower over the other man. 'Outside, Freed,' he ordered. 'I don't intend giving the other patrons the satisfaction of seeing me hit you.'

'No,' Nicholas sneered. 'I suppose you've had enough adverse publicity to last you a lifetime.'

'Meaning?' Joel said dangerously soft.

'Don't pretend you don't know, Brent. You and that little——'

'That does it!' Joel launched the other man to his feet and dragged him outside.

Sabina and Nancy stood up together, quickly following them. 'Oh God!' Sabina groaned. 'I hope he doesn't hurt him.'

'Joel can look after himself,' Nancy assured her.

Sabina shot her a quick glance, colour flooding her cheeks. 'I meant Nicholas.'

'Did you?'

'Yes!'

Nancy patted her hand. 'One day you'll have to sit down and tell me exactly what you feel for Nick, and for Joel, of course.'

'I don't feel anything for Joel! I hardly know him. I——'

'Not now, Sabina. We'd better go and see what he's done to that hot-headed husband of mine.'

Sabina didn't bother to correct this last statement, too anxious to find out what was happening outside to worry about such trivia. Joel was alone when they got outside.

He turned to face them with a satisfied smile. 'That takes care of that,' he grinned.

'What have you done with him?' Nancy asked worriedly.

'Sent him home to bed.'

'Did you hit him?' Sabina demanded to know. The mood Nicholas had been in he certainly wouldn't have gone willingly.

'I didn't need to,' Joel still smiled. 'The fresh air

knocked him out for me. I got one of the club drivers to take him home.'

Sabina frowned. 'Driver . . .? I didn't know they had drivers.'

'At least that proves Freed doesn't make a habit of this sort of thing.'

'Of course he doesn't!' Nancy was indignant.

'There's no of course about it,' Joel frowned. 'He should be being put to bed about now.' He held up some car keys. 'I took the liberty of borrowing these. I don't think he'll miss them,' he added with amusement. 'I'll drive you both home.'

'You can drop me off first,' Nancy told him once they were in the car. 'I only live round the corner.'

'Oh, but——'

'Certainly,' Joel cut in on Sabina's protest. 'And don't worry about Nicholas. The only thing he'll have tomorrow is a hangover.'

'He doesn't usually drink like that.' Nancy chewed her bottom lip. 'Oh, lord!' she suddenly went pale. 'I've left my ring at the club.'

Joel shook his head. 'Nicholas pocketed it.'

'Oh.'

'Maybe he'll give it to you now, Sabina,' he taunted her as she sat in the back.

'Ha, ha!' she glared at him in the driving mirror.

'He'd better not,' Nancy said fiercely.

'I'm sure he won't,' Joel told her gently.

She frowned. 'Then why has he taken it?'

Sabina was wondering the same thing, although right now she had more important things on her mind. If Joel was dropping Nancy off first that meant she was going to be alone with him on the drive to her own home.

CHAPTER NINE

'YOU'RE very quiet.'

Sabina turned to find Joel looking down at her. They had arrived outside her apartment block a few minutes earlier, and she hadn't yet found the strength to get out of the car and leave him.

His hand moved along the back of her seat to caress her nape. 'What's wrong, Sabina?' he asked huskily.

Her eyes glowed deeply green in the darkness. 'Why did you do it, Joel?' she asked breathlessly.

'Do what?'

'Deliberately set out to antagonise Nicholas. And don't say you didn't, because I know you did.'

He shrugged. 'I thought it was the other way round. He was ever so slightly drunk.'

'Because of you,' she accused.

Joel shook his head. 'Not because of me. Can't you see what's in front of your eyes?'

'What do you mean?' Her tone was sharp.

He sighed. 'Never mind, I'm sure the situation will right itself. I'll make sure it does,' he added grimly. 'But in the meantime . . .' he bent his head and claimed her lips with his own.

Sabina fought against this drugging seduction. 'Joel, no!' she tried to push him away. 'This has to stop,' she said desperately. 'Joel . . .'

'Kiss me, woman, and be quiet,' he growled, his lips at her throat, his hands caressing her creamy skin.

'But, Joel——'

'I hate women who argue,' he murmured impatiently.

'Now kiss me. Open your mouth and——'

'Did Nicole argue?' she hit out, fighting for her sanity as his hand moved into the low neckline of her gown to caress her breast, bringing the nipple to full pulsating life.

He slowly moved back to look at her, his hand instantly removed. 'You're trying to anger me,' he frowned. 'Why?'

Because she was terrified, terrified of her own weakness towards him. No matter how she felt about it she had to marry Nicholas, and being in Joel's arms like this was absolute torture for her, reminding her of all she would be sacrificing when she became Nicholas's wife in a week's time.

'Sabina?' Joel gently shook her.

'You're taking advantage of me,' she accused weakly.

'*I'm* taking advantage of *you*?' he scorned. 'You know damn well I can't keep my hands off you.'

'I won't have an affair with you, Joel,' she told him quietly. 'I couldn't do that.'

'You offered in Scotland.'

'That was when——' she broke off, biting her lip as she turned away from his searching eyes.

Joel wrenched her face back round, his hand rough on her chin. 'When . . .?' he prompted.

She shook her head. 'It doesn't matter.'

'Tell me, damn you!' he shook her hard. 'Or let me tell you. In Scotland you'd decided to call off your wedding to Freed. And yet you haven't. *Why* haven't you?'

'That's none of your business!'

'I'm making it my business,' Joel told her firmly. 'In Scotland I thought you were marrying Freed for his money, but finding out you were Charles Smith's daughter made that highly unlikely.' His grey eyes narrowed on her pale face. 'Or does it?' he said thoughtfully. 'Sabina, is your father in some sort of trouble? Is that your reason for not backing out of the marriage?'

'Don't be silly,' she forced a lightness to her tone. 'My father is very rich.'

'It doesn't necessarily have to be financial, I suppose,' Joel mused. 'Freed and your father are in business together——'

'Only as regards the newspaper,' Sabina put in hastily.

'Mm, I wonder . . . Sabina, is——'

'There's nothing wrong!' she said sharply. 'Now just leave me alone.' The arced beam of another car's headlights illuminated them before pulling up behind them. 'I have to go now. I—I'll see you tomorrow, won't I?'

'To look at the other houses,' he nodded. 'But you'll come and see Satan first.'

'*No*, I can't!' She had to stop being alone with him, had to stop——

'I'm worried about him,' Joel softly interrupted her thoughts.

'Worried? What's wrong with him?'

He shrugged. 'I have no idea. He keeps wrecking the place.'

'That wouldn't be difficult,' Sabina remarked dryly, remembering the chaos she had walked in on this afternoon.

'Cheeky!' Joel grinned. 'I haven't moved a thing since your tidy-up. But Satan has, he keeps throwing things out of cupboards, and then growling at me when I throw *him* out.'

Sabina frowned. 'I hope he isn't ill. I wouldn't——' The car door swung open beside her and she turned in surprise to see her father standing there. She almost groaned out loud, realising it must have been him in the car behind them. 'Daddy,' she greeted dully as he bent down.

He smiled at her. 'I just came to tell Nicholas—My God!' his eyes widened as he took in Sabina sitting in the circle of Joel Brent's arms. 'What are you doing here? Isn't this Nicholas's car?' Her father sounded puzzled now.

'It is,' Joel confirmed lazily. 'I'm afraid your partner was drunk and disorderly, so I brought your daughter home.'

'Sabina?' her father looked uncertain.

'It's true, Daddy. Nicholas—he wasn't at all himself tonight.'

'He was stoned,' Joel said dryly.

Her father looked angry. 'I don't believe that.'

'He was, Daddy.'

'So would any man be when in the company of his ex-wife and his future wife.' Joel sounded amused.

'You saw Nancy tonight?' Sabina's father gasped.

'I was with her,' Joel drawled.

Her father shook his head dazedly. 'I don't understand any of this.'

'Perhaps I should come inside and we can talk about it,' Joel suggested. 'There are a couple of other things I should like to discuss with you, Mr Smith.'

'That *you* would like to discuss with *me*?' her father exploded, his face red with anger. 'I'd like to know a few things myself, like what you were doing in Scotland with Sabina? Don't you realise that if Nicholas found out about you two he'd call off the wedding? And now you're with him again, Sabina,' her father turned on her accusingly.

'Correction,' Joel drawled mockingly, 'I'm with her.

I'm sure that if Sabina had a choice she would rather be elsewhere.'

She certainly would! This whole situation was turning out to be a nightmare. 'Too true,' she agreed grimly. 'Would you mind moving and letting me out of the car, Daddy,' she said impatiently.

He stood back. 'What about Nicholas's car?'

Joel swung out from behind the wheel, joining the two of them on the pavement. 'I'll leave it here and get a taxi. Unless you feel like driving me home, Sabina?' he slanted her a taunting look.

Her father took a firm hold of her arm. 'She isn't going anywhere with you. Why don't you stay out of her life and stop trying to cause trouble?'

'Am I causing trouble?'

'You know you are.' Sabina's father held her against his side. 'She's going to marry Nicholas.'

Dark eyebrows rose arrogantly. 'Are you sure about that?'

'If you do anything to prevent it I'll ruin you, Brent!'

'With the photo-copies you have of personal letters of mine?' Joel rasped.

'Daddy, please——'

'Stay out of this, Sabina,' he ordered.

'It seems to be the habit of the men in your life to try and silence you,' Joel taunted her. 'Whose method do you prefer?'

Sabina blushed, glaring at him as he gave a throaty chuckle. 'Could we go inside now, Daddy?' She put a hand up to her temple. 'I have a headache.'

He gave her a probing look. 'You haven't been drinking too, have you?'

'I didn't get your daughter drunk so that she would spend time with me,' Joel drawled. 'I don't need to.'

'I'm sure you don't,' her father snapped angrily. 'Why

the hell she's infatuated with you I'll——'

'Daddy!' Sabina gasped. 'I am not infatuated with him!' Her face was fiery red, her body stiff.

'No, she isn't,' Joel agreed grimly.

'No, I'm not,' she insisted needlessly. 'Now can we go inside, Dad?' she said impatiently.

'Okay, let's go, Sabina. And I'll thank you to stay out of her life in future,' her father told Joel. 'Can't you see you're just upsetting her.'

'I don't think she's "upset" by seeing me,' Joel antagonised. 'I think that's the last word I would use to describe her reaction to me.'

Sabina had heard enough, and she wrenched away from her father to glare rebelliously at both of them. 'I'm going inside,' she said angrily. 'You can continue this conversation if you want to, but I've heard enough!' She turned on her heel and walked off.

'Sabina . . .'

She stopped at the sound of Joel's voice. 'Yes?' she didn't turn.

'Ten o'clock tomorrow,' he reminded her softly.

She spun round, her eyes wide. 'You still want to go?'

'But of course.' He held out the car keys to Sabina's father. 'Give these to your partner. We'll continue our own interesting conversation some other time.' It was a threat, not a promise.

It didn't take Sabina's father long to catch up with her. 'Where are you going with Brent at ten o'clock tomorrow?' he demanded to know.

'Wait until we get inside,' she said impatiently, managing to smile at the manservant as he let them into the apartment.

'Well?' her father's stance was challenging.

'Have I ever questioned you about your friends?' Sabina counter-challenged. 'Well, have I?'

'It's hardly the same thing,' he blustered. 'I'm your father, and——'

'Then perhaps you should set an example for me. Which one was it tonight, Dawn or Sybil?' She knew that her father was escorting two models at the moment, although neither knew about the other. If they had they would have scratched each other's eyes out.

'Don't be facetious!'

'It was Dawn. She always puts you in this overbearing mood. My, how she must pander to your ego!'

'We were talking about you,' he reminded her thunderously.

'*You* were talking about me.' She walked over to her bedroom, yawning tiredly. 'Goodnight, Dad.'

'Sabina!'

'I'm tired, and I mustn't be up late, not if I'm to be ready when Joel arrives at ten o'clock.' The last was added to infuriate her father, and by the angry tide of red colour that washed over his face she thought she had succeeded. Good, he wasn't exactly blameless in this mess she was involved in, and she wouldn't allow him to get off scot-free.

'But Nicholas——'

'Behaved disgracefully this evening. Look,' she sighed, 'I don't want to talk about it any more.'

'But what was Nancy Freed doing with you tonight?'

'She wasn't with me, she was with Joel. But then he already told you that.' She yawned exaggeratedly. 'I'll see you in the morning.'

Once in her bedroom she leant back against the door. What an evening it had been, a total disaster as regarded Nicholas and herself. Well, he was going to have a hangover in the morning. And that certainly wouldn't improve his temper.

*

Her father was still at the breakfast table when she came out of her room the next morning, and considering it was already nine o'clock he should have left for his office long ago. The reason for his delay this morning soon became obvious.

'I don't want you to go out with Brent today,' he said as soon as he sat down at the table.

She poured herself some coffee. 'Your disapproval is duly noted.' She sipped her hot drink.

'And ignored!' He scowled heavily. 'Damn it, Sabina, you can't go out with him when you're marrying Nicholas.'

She sighed. 'I'm helping him find a house, that's all.'

'A house? But—You aren't moving in with him, are you?'

His shock made her laugh. 'I already have, once.'

He stood up to pace the room. 'It can't go on, Sabina. If Nicholas should find out——'

'He already knows,' she took great pleasure in informing him. 'Now I really think you should go to work. If Nicholas is already there his temper won't be improved by your lateness. Besides, he could be wondering about his car.'

'I checked, he isn't in yet either, and I doubt he will be if he drank as much as Brent said he did.'

'Oh, he did.'

'Oh God,' he came to stand in front of her, 'have you driven him to drink now?'

'Not me.' Sabina stood up, her cup of coffee in her hand. 'His ex-wife did that.'

'Nancy? But—Where are you going?' her father demanded as she walked away.

'To my room. To get washed and then dressed. Really, Dad, what a silly question!' she shook her head mockingly.

He frowned darkly. 'You're altogether too cheeky lately. You never used to be like this,' he said complainingly. 'I don't know what's come over you.'

'You have!' her eyes flashed. 'I've finally realised what a bossy, domineering man you really are. You're utterly selfish too. Nicholas already knew about your borrowing from Chesnick, but he——'

Her father was pale. 'He knows?'

'Oh yes. But even if he hadn't he would have done. You see, I told him. That was when he said he already knew. I don't think it had even occurred to him until that moment that he could use it to hold me. It would take a devious schemer like you to think of something like that. Well, he has the idea now, and until I become his wife he's going to keep it. I hope you're proud of yourself!' She slammed into her bedroom and locked the door behind her.

Her father was right, she hadn't used to behave like this. Loving Joel had changed her, made her hate being engaged to Nicholas, made her long to go back to Scotland as Joel as suggested they should.

Joel arrived exactly at ten o'clock. Fortunately her father had already left for the office. She didn't want another scene, and the determination in Joel's face told her he had been ready for one.

'He's gone to work,' she told him mockingly, putting the finishing touches to her make-up, adding the coral lipstick. She was dressed in a black crushed-velvet skirt and white fitted blouse, her hair in a bun at her nape. She looked cool and composed.

In contrast to her Joel had on faded denims and a matching denim shirt. 'Are you going on somewhere?' he eyed her tauntingly.

She flushed, facing him, her chin held high. 'I'm trying to look the part of a respectable house-buyer,' she told him in a stilted voice, knowing her real reason had been to give herself confidence against Joel's blatant masculinity. It was even more apparent in those casual clothes, the shirt taut across his chest, the denim trousers low down on his hips.

Joel sat down in one of the armchairs. 'Go and change,' he ordered. 'I'll wait for you.'

Her eyes widened indignantly. 'I will not! I look perfectly respectable.'

'You look—charming,' his eyes were deeply grey. 'Beautiful, in fact. But for the moment I think you would be more comfortable in trousers. You can put on something beautiful later on.'

'I'd rather stay as I am.'

'I'm sure you would.' He slowly stood up, moving to stand in front of her. 'And later on you can put on something really feminine for me. But for now I'd prefer to see you as I first saw you.' His hand moved up to remove the pins from her hair, threading through the blonde tresses to release them about her shoulders. 'You shouldn't put your hair up like that, it just tempts me to do this.' He bent his head with a groan, claiming her lips with his own. 'I missed you last night,' he murmured against her mouth. 'I missed you being with me, sharing my bedroom, if not my bed.'

'Joel . . .'

'Go and change,' he repeated. 'Put on a pair of those tight denims you used to wear at the cottage, and let me torture myself looking at you.'

Sabina had to laugh at his pained expression. 'If I stay like this you won't need to suffer.'

'I think I can stand the pain.'

Still laughing, she went into the bedroom to change, choosing her newest pair of denims, the pair she had shrunk only last week and not worn yet. With them she put on a body-hugging red sun-top, her arms and shoulders bare. By the time she had combed her hair loose she looked vastly different from the elegant young lady who had greeted Joel only fifteen minutes earlier.

'God, what a pleasable pain!' were Joel's first words. He took a deep breath. 'Right, let's go, Satan is expecting us.'

'How is he today?' asked Sabina once they were outside in the car.

'The same. He was hiding under the bed when I came out. I'll just have to get him out of London as soon as possible.'

'He hates it here as much as I do.'

'As much as we all do. Do you miss the cottage, Sabina?'

Did she! She would give anything to be back there. 'I don't think about it,' she lied.

'Have you heard from Freed today?'

She stiffened. 'No.'

'Why do you suppose he got drunk last night?'

'I have no idea.'

'None?'

'No!' her voice was sharp.

'Is he in love with you?'

'What is this, Joel?' she became aggressive. 'Twenty questions?'

'And the rest,' he said grimly. 'There's so much I want to know it will take a hell of a lot more than twenty questions. Did you know before last night that Freed is still in love with his ex-wife?'

'Now that I don't believe,' Sabina shook her head.

'Don't or won't?'

'Don't,' Sabina said firmly. 'Did you know that Nancy still loved him?'

'No, but I do now,' he acknowledged dryly. 'All the

ingredients for a happy ending. So why isn't it?'

She shrugged, 'You tell me.'

'All right, I will. You.'

'Me?' she frowned.

'Yes, you. You're in the way of their happiness, hanging on to Freed's ring for grim death.'

'I—I'm not!' she spluttered at the injustice of his words. 'I don't—I wouldn't——'

'You wouldn't what? For God's sake, Sabina, you have no right marrying him when you respond to me as you do. You have no right marrying anyone when it's me you want.'

'You? But I—I——'

'Don't lie, Sabina, not now. I'm getting to the stage where I'm going to say to hell with your engagement, to hell with Freed, and I'm going to take you to my bed right now. What would you do if I did that?'

'I'm—I've never slept with anyone, Joel.' She licked her lips nervously.

'I know that,' his hand fleetingly touched her cheek. 'That just makes it more important that I be your first lover, the all-important first lover who's never forgotten.'

'You—you want me like that?'

'You know I do, I've been telling you so for days.'

'But Joel——'

'This is hardly the place for such a conversation.' He stopped the car and came round to open her door for her. 'Let's talk inside.'

Joel's apartment was as tidy as she had left it yesterday. 'Where's Satan?' she asked to cover her nervousness, shaken by what he had just said to her.

'Probably under the bed where I left him.' Joel put out his hand to her. 'Come with me?'

Sabina was aware of the importance of the request.

Joel wasn't just asking her to enter the bedroom with him, he was asking her to commit herself to him, body and soul.

'Sabina?' he prompted huskily.

She put her hand in his, her bottom lip trembling as she felt his strong fingers close about hers. 'Yes, Joel,' she smiled tremulously.

He drew a ragged breath. 'I was hoping that would be your answer. Right, let's go and see this cat of ours. I couldn't get near him this morning, let's hope you have more luck with him.'

All her pleadings for Satan to come out met stony silence from him. Not even a growl came from the darkness under the bed. Sabina put a tentative hand out towards him, and received a hiss and a scratch for her trouble.

She stood up, nursing her injured hand. 'Ouch!' she grimaced.

Joel was sitting on the bed. He took hold of her hand to look at the scratch, lifting it to slowly kiss the sore and ragged flesh, his eyes intent on her face as he pulled her towards him, holding her captive between his splayed legs, kissing the bareness of her shoulder, the hollow between her breasts.

'I'll let you get close to me,' he murmured throatily. 'As close as you like.' He caressed her shoulders. 'How close would you like to be, Sabina?'

'Very close,' she admitted huskily. 'Oh, Joel, I love you,' she told him brokenly. 'I love you so much. Please believe me!' Tears welled up in her deep green eyes.

'I believe you,' he cupped each side of her face with his hands. 'Now you believe me when I tell you I'm not letting you marry Freed. In fact,' he lifted her left hand, 'his ring can come off right now.' He pulled it from her finger and went to throw it across the room.

'No!' Sabina stopped him. 'I—You don't understand.
I must marry Nicholas.'

Joel became suddenly still. 'Why?'

She bit her lip, her eyes dark with pain. 'I just have
to.'

'Tell me!' he ordered tautly.

She gave him an agonised look, turning away. 'I
can't!'

'Why can't you?'

'Because it isn't my secret to tell.'

He stood up. 'Then it's Freed's. We'll go and see him,
right now, and sort this out. But whatever happens,
whatever hold he has over you, you are not marrying
him. Understood?'

She followed him as he strode out of the bedroom,
his grim expression indicative of his dark mood. 'But,
Joel——'

He turned so suddenly she almost walked into the
back of him. He shook her hard, his fingers painful in
her flesh. 'Do you understand?'

'Yes—but you don't. You see, it isn't only Nicholas
and I involved——'

'No, it's Nancy and me too.'

'That wasn't what I meant. Although as your future
wife of course she's involved.'

'I only told you I was getting married, I didn't say
Nancy was the woman involved.' Joel led the way out
of the building to his parked car. 'Direct me to Freed's,'
he ordered once they were inside.

She did so. 'But if you aren't marrying Nancy,' she
frowned, 'who——' her eyes widened as he turned to
give her a meaningful look. 'Me?' she squeaked disbelievingly. 'You mean me?'

'I mean you,' he nodded. 'What do you think my
interest in you has all been about?'

'I didn't know. I just thought—*Marriage*, Joel?' she gasped.

'Marriage,' he confirmed. 'My ring on your finger. You belonging to me for all time. Do you want that?'

'Oh yes!'

'Then that's the way it's going to be. I have the licence, the time, all I needed was the girl's consent. I have that?'

'Yes.' But he hadn't said he loved her! She pushed this thought to the back of her mind. 'What day, Joel? What time?'

'Today. At four o'clock.'

'Today?'

He nodded. 'Today.'

'But I thought we were going to look at houses,' she protested dazedly.

'Did you like the house we looked at yesterday?'

'I loved it.'

'Good,' there was a wealth of satisfaction in his voice. 'Because I bought it.'

'But you said——'

'I had to make sure you met me today. Of course the house won't be ready to move into for another few weeks, but we can stay at the cottage until then. You like that idea?'

'I love it. And so will Satan.'

'Ah yes, Satan. He has good taste in women. He liked you straight away.'

'I have a scar on my ankle to prove he didn't,' she said ruefully. 'Joel, at the house you said I would want to look after the children myself—did you mean it?'

'That's your way, isn't it?'

'Yes. But how did you know that?'

He stopped the car outside Nicholas's home, turning to look at her. 'I know you. Now let's go and see Freed.

The advent of children into our life can be discussed in more congenial surroundings, tonight,' he added throatily.

Tonight, when she would be his wife. But would Nicholas release her?

They were shown into the lounge by Nicholas's housekeeper, Nicholas emerging from his bedroom a few minutes later. He winced as the daylight hit his sensitive eyes. 'What time is it?' he asked groggily.

'Eleven o'clock,' Joel supplied. 'Hangover, Freed?' he asked callously.

Nicholas gave him a baleful look. 'You sarcastic bastard,' he snapped. 'I ought to——'

'Nick!'

They all turned to see Nancy Freed standing in the doorway, dressed only in a man's towelling robe, Nicholas's towelling robe.

CHAPTER TEN

NANCY laughed at their expressions. 'Well, don't look so surprised—I've only spent the night with my husband! At least, he will be, as soon as we're able to make it legal again. But in the meantime,' she held out her hand, her wedding band back on her finger, 'at least I have this back where it belongs.' She put her arm through Nicholas's. 'Anyone care to come to a wedding?' she asked them gaily.

'Snap,' Joel drawled.

'Snap?' Nancy looked from Sabina to Joel. 'Are you two . . .?'

'Yes,' Joel answered her. 'Once I've sorted out with Nicholas why Sabina thought she *had* to marry him.' His narrowed gaze levelled on the other man.

'Don't look at me,' Nicholas instantly denied responsibility, sitting down with a groan. 'God, my head aches!'

'I'll go and get you one of my remedies, darling,' Nancy instantly offered. 'That is, if you think Mrs Jones will let me into the kitchen. She looked scandalised this morning when she saw me in your bed.'

Nicholas caught her hand as she walked past him. 'You won't be long?' his voice was husky.

'No,' she promised softly.

All brittle sophistication had left the other woman, her love now unhidden for her husband. Sabina felt a glow begin inside her, a feeling that everything was going to be all right for her and Joel too. If only he had told her he loved her, even if it weren't true!

'I believe this belongs to you.' Joel held out Sabina's engagement ring to Nicholas. 'She won't be needing it.'

'So I gathered,' he said dryly. 'Keep it,' he told her. 'A memento of an old man's folly.'

'Nicholas——'

'It's all right, my dear,' he smiled at her. 'I have what I want, which is Nancy back at my side, and you seem to have what you want. I can't say I approve of my replacement . . .' he gave Joel a taunting look, 'but if you love him he can't be all bad.'

Sabina smiled at Joel's thunderous look, knowing Nicholas was enjoying baiting him. 'He isn't bad at all,' she said huskily. 'And I'm so pleased about you and Nancy.'

'So am I, Sabina, so am I. Let's hope we make a better job of it the second time around. And just for the record, Joel, I am not a wife-beater,' he added mockingly. 'As I'm sure Nancy will confirm.'

'I already gathered that,' Joel said dryly.

'She's told me everything,' Nicholas said with a sigh. 'That there was no affair between you two, that she even told you I hit her to try and gain your interest. You knew about that too, didn't you, Sabina?'

'Er—yes.'

'Then what the *hell* were you doing marrying me?' he asked dumbfoundedly. 'You should run away from men who use brute force. Oh, I struck out and accidentally caught Nancy on the side of the cheek, but it was when that happened that I realised I had to get out.'

'How can you be so sure the marriage will work a second time?' Joel asked sceptically.

Nicholas shrugged. 'I can't. Just as you can't be certain your marriage will work a first time. But a word of advice, Joel, even though I know you don't want it, if a woman is insecure in your love then you'll lose her.

Nancy was jealous of my first wife, couldn't understand how I'd loved another woman before her. It isn't easy to make them understand that you love each of them a different way.'

Sabina wasn't even sure that Joel did love her, let alone in what way. Nicole Dupont still seemed to be such an important part of his life. She was his 'girl who went away', and no one could compete with a dead woman, not even a wife.

'I'll remember,' Joel drawled. 'So why did Sabina have to marry you?'

'She didn't. At least, not as far as I was concerned. Her father put the idea into her head, I just played along with it. Sabina would have made me an ideal wife.'

Grey eyes levelled on her. 'Well?'

'I thought—Daddy said—You see, Nicholas—Oh, I just don't know any more!' She sat down before she fell down.

'Nicholas?'

He sighed. 'Charles had some incredible idea that I was going to ruin him if Sabina didn't marry me.'

'And were you?' There was a steely edge to Joel's voice.

'No, damn it!' Nicholas denied heatedly. 'We've been partners too long for that. Oh, you might as well know, you're going to be his son-in-law, Charles has been dipping his fingers into the Chasnick coffers. I knew about it, of course. But I also knew that Charles is a good enough businessman to get himself out of trouble. It never crossed my mind to bring pressure to bear where Sabina is concerned.'

'But it crossed his,' Joel said thoughtfully.

'It would appear so,' Nicholas nodded. 'The first I knew of it was when Sabina got back from Bedfordshire.'

Joel frowned. 'Bedfordshire? When did you go there?'

Sabina swallowed hard, her face pale. 'I——'

'About seven weeks ago,' Nicholas cut in. 'She went away to think things out. When she came back she came out with this ridiculous idea that I meant to ruin her father. It was too late to call off the wedding without causing a sensation, and so I just let things ride.'

'Bedfordshire?' Joel repeated tauntingly. 'Couldn't you have thought of something better than that?' he mocked her.

Colour flooded her cheeks. 'It was my father's explanation, not mine.'

'Again?' Joel snapped. 'My God, that man has a lot to answer for! I'll be glad when we're married and away from here.'

Nicholas's eyes widened. 'You're leaving London?'

'Tomorrow,' Joel confirmed. 'We're going to Scotland. Which, incidentally, is where Sabina was seven weeks ago.'

'Joel!' she gasped, looking in embarrassment at Nicholas.

'Were you?' he asked with some amusement.

'Yes,' she admitted miserably.

'With Joel?'

'I——'

'Yes,' Joel answered for her, eyes narrowed in challenge as he looked at the other man.

Nicholas spluttered with laughter. 'Good for you, Sabina! You're good for her, Joel. She always let her father run her life for her, I can see how she's changed this last few weeks.'

Nancy came in from the kitchen, a glassful of dark red fluid in her hand. 'Here you are, my darling,' she smiled at Nicholas. 'You'll feel much better after this.'

'Ugh!' he grimaced after the first tentative sip. 'What's in it?'

'Don't ask!' she chuckled. 'Just drink it down and within ten minutes I guarantee you'll feel on top of the world. Go on, drink it. All of it.' She took the empty glass from him. 'Now, have I missed anything interesting?'

'Just some straightening out that needed to be done,' Joel answered her. 'Now, about that wedding——'

Nancy sat on the arm of Nicholas's chair. 'When is it? We would love to come, wouldn't we, Nick?'

'I wouldn't miss it for the world,' he confirmed. 'But in the meantime we'll have to cancel next week's wedding.'

'Not necessarily,' Joel said thoughtfully. 'Why don't the two of you use that date instead? You've got time to get a licence, and everything else is arranged.'

Nancy's eyes glowed. 'I think that's a lovely idea. Nick?'

'Suits me. I don't know what was in that drink, but I feel better already.'

'Good, because we need you at the wedding this afternoon,' Joel told him. 'You and Nancy can act as our witnesses.'

'Today?' Nicholas spluttered. 'Good God, man, you're a fast worker! And what if I hadn't been willing to release her?'

'I would have taken her anyway,' he was arrogantly told. 'She belongs to me.'

'Charming!' Nancy grimaced. 'We aren't a possession, you know.'

Flinty eyes were turned on Sabina. 'Well?' Joel asked her haughtily.

She moved to his side, relaxing against him as he put his arm about her waist. 'He's right, I do belong to him,' she said huskily.

'Start as you mean to go on, Sabina,' Nancy advised,

'and don't let him walk all over you. I know this brute
of a man you're marrying, and he likes to have everything his own way. You'll never get anywhere by giving
in to him.'

Joel smiled. 'There are ways and ways, Nancy. Sabina
is well aware of my vulnerability towards her.'

'Really?' Nancy said interestedly. 'Tell me more.'

He gave a throaty laugh. 'Censored, I'm afraid. But
I'm sure Sabina will be the first to admit that with her
I've had nothing my own way.'

'Well, Sabina?' Nancy's eyes danced mischievously.
'Has he or hasn't he?'

'I'm keeping quiet,' she said shyly. 'Joel, I think we
should go and see my father. I can't get married without
him being there.'

'We'll talk to him together. We'll call for you about
three-thirty,' he told the other couple.

To say her father was surprised by this sudden turn
of events was putting it mildly; he was stunned.
'Married?' he gasped. 'You two are getting *married*?'

'We are,' Joel told him arrogantly. 'Nicholas has very
kindly released her from any commitment to him.'

Sabina was sure that her father hadn't imagined such
an occurrence when she had telephoned him and asked
him to come home. The poor man looked dazed by the
whole thing. 'Daddy,' she said gently, 'everything is all
right with Nicholas. He and Nancy are getting married
again.'

'They are?' He looked even more startled. 'And you're
going to marry my daughter?' he asked Joel.

'I am,' Joel replied haughtily.

Her father looked at her. 'You want to marry him?'

'Yes, Daddy.'

'Then I'm happy for you. I've only ever wanted your
happiness, Sabina.'

'And you think she would have been happy married to Freed?' Joel snorted.

Her father's head went back, his gaze unflinching. 'She would always have had financial security married to him. I had no idea you wanted to marry her, or I would never have tried to interfere. Your time together seemed to me to be a temporary thing. With Nicholas she would never have needed to worry about her future, he never takes the risks I do.'

Sabina frowned. 'Is that the reason . . .?

He sighed. 'This last setback made me aware of my own failings. I just wanted to secure your future.'

'Oh, Daddy!' She went into his arms, feeling herself cocooned in his love, the love that had driven him to such desperate measures.

'I believe I can offer her the same security,' Joel told her father softly.

Her father held her at arm's length. 'I've been wrong, so very wrong. I think love is the only security Sabina needs. All I ask is that you take care of her and love her.'

But love was a security Joel hadn't offered, and didn't offer, not before the marriage ceremony or after it. The marriage ceremony itself was short and unemotional, and the dinner party her father insisted on giving afterwards seemed to pass as if in a dream.

And then they were alone in Joel's apartment—*their* apartment—a sudden tension rising up between them as Sabina realised she had given herself to this man for life, had committed her love to him for all time, and he hadn't once said he loved her in return. Perhaps he didn't, perhaps he just wanted her. As long as he continued to want her, she thought, that would be enough.

'Sabina.'

She looked up at Joel, her eyes suddenly very wide and frightened. It was late. They had been listening to records for the last hour, not Joel's because he said he couldn't bear to listen to himself, and now it was time for bed, time for them to go into the bedroom and share the bed as man and wife. And Sabina was petrified.

'Yes?' she asked huskily.

'Sabina, twice today I've been told that as long as I love you I'll never lose you. And yet you haven't once asked if I love you.' He frowned. 'You've told me you love me, and yet you don't ask for love in return.'

She licked her lips, facing him across the distance of the hearthrug, their chairs opposite each other. It had been this way since their return, no contact, only polite conversation. And she didn't know how much longer she could stand it.

'You can't ask for love,' she replied finally. 'It's either given or it isn't.'

'Do you know why I haven't told you I love you?' He was watching her intently.

Her head went back, only the slight tremble of her lower lip betraying her vulnerability. 'Because you don't, I suppose,' she said lightly, her lip trembling even more.

Joel shook his head. 'It isn't that at all.' He came down on his knees in front of her, taking her hand into his. 'I haven't told you because I love you too much to be able to put it into simple words. If I tell you that without you my life means nothing, that when you aren't with me the sun ceases to shine, that when you left me in Scotland I thought I would die, that I *did* die until I saw you again. Seeing you at the concert hall every day brought me back to life again. So now you know,' he said heavily. 'If you ever go away from me again I'll just give up living.'

'Joel . . .' she choked, too moved to speak for several minutes. 'That song. The song——'

'The Girl Who Went Away?' he finished. 'You. That's why I wanted it taken out of the concert. It's one thing to pour your heart out to an audience, another thing to do it to the girl in question, especially when she's wearing someone else's ring.'

'But you said that girl no longer existed.'

'We'd just argued,' he sighed. 'The girl in London no longer seemed like the girl I'd come to love. But later on at the party I knew you were still the same, that deep inside you still loved me too.'

'I thought the song was for Nicole.'

'Yes—Nicole,' he said heavily. 'I suppose we have to talk about her.' He pulled Sabina down on to the carpet with him, sitting with his arm about her shoulders as they leant back against the chair.

'All I need to know is if you loved her as much as you now love me.'

'Love!' Joel gave a shout of bitter laughter. 'I didn't love her at all.'

Sabina's eyes widened. 'But——'

'Not at all,' he repeated firmly. 'I never did.'

'But everyone said you were going to marry her.'

'I know,' he sighed. 'But by that time she was dead, so why should I bother to deny it?'

'You could have denied it to me! I've been thinking all sorts of things about the two of you. I even imagined that room in the cottage was a miniature shrine to her. I couldn't believe it when I saw the piano, the music sheets.' Sabina shook her head. 'All that time you'd been writing music, and I thought you'd been shutting yourself in with her. I thought you loved her.'

'I told you, never. I'll talk about her this once, and then no more. All right?' Joel waited for her nod of confirmation. 'I went out with Nicole for a few months, until I realised she couldn't get through the day without drugs. I've never liked that scene, or the people in it. Exit Nicole. Only she had other ideas. Wherever I went she was there too. I finally decided to talk it out with her once and for all. I agreed to let her drive me back from a concert one night. Note, I agreed to let *her* drive.'

'She was driving that night?' Sabina asked breathlessly.

'Yes.' He sighed. 'She thought she could fly the damned thing. Needless to say she couldn't. You can't believe how beautiful she was, Sabina. So beautiful, and yet so damned corrupt.'

She knew exactly how beautiful the other woman had been, and she could also mourn the destruction of such beauty with drugs. 'She was very young.'

'Twenty-six,' he nodded. 'So I went to Scotland to try and sort my own life out. I found peace there, clean air to breathe, time to think. I also found you.'

'You seemed to dislike me.'

'Never. Not even when I really thought you were a reporter. I was having trouble keeping my hands off you, and frustration is never conducive to a man's temper. When you disappeared . . .! God,' he groaned, 'I never want to go through a time like that again.'

'I wanted to come back, but I was afraid my father would drag up all the speculation attached to the crash, that he would make things awkward for you again.'

'Your father's protection amounted almost to blackmail,' he scowled. 'He had the right idea, but the wrong method. As you know, I stayed in Scotland. I wrote that damned song——'

Sabina put her fingers over his lips. 'Lovely, lovely song,' she said huskily.

'Maybe,' he kissed her fingertips, keeping her hand in his. 'When it became clear you weren't coming back I came to London to sort out the concert my agent had been organising. Then you appeared again, destroying my peace of mind, and I determined to get you for myself, any way I could.' He stood up, holding out his hand to her. 'Coming to bed now?'

She went into his arms, resting her head on his chest, his heartbeat sounding like a bass drum in her ear. 'Tell me you love me, Joel. Just once say "I love you, Sabina", and I'll never ask again.'

'I'll tell you as I make love to you,' he promised softly. 'With my lips and body I'll tell you.'

To be made love to by Joel must be the most beautiful experience any woman could have, his desire to give her pleasure completely selfless. He didn't rush her, kissing and caressing her until she felt on fire for him.

'Joel,' she breathed raggedly, his lips at her breasts. 'Joel, I want to please you too. Show me how, darling. Please!'

'Not this time, my love,' he groaned. 'I can't hold back any longer.'

He soothed her initial pain, murmuring words of love until trembling desire invaded every part of her, rising to a crescendo until she and Joel reached the ultimate pleasure together. No more words were spoken as they slowly drifted off to sleep in each other's arms.

The next morning Joel lay against her breasts, their legs still entwined.

'No woman had ever—I've never—Thank you, my darling,' he said emotionally. 'Thank you for giving me your innocence. I never thought any woman would give me such a gift.'

Sabina smoothed his hair. 'I'm glad it happened this

way too, glad——' She broke off as the doorbell began
to ring.

'What the hell——!' Joel sat up, the sleepy passion
fading from his eyes. 'Who could be calling this time of
day? It's barely eight-thirty.' He scowled, getting out of
bed to pull on a robe. 'Don't move,' he ordered. I'll be
right back,' he promised deeply. 'Some people have no
tact,' he snapped as the doorbell rang again.

'Have pity, Joel,' Sabina giggled at his anger. 'They
don't realise you were just about to make love to your
wife.'

'I was going to spend the day in bed with my wife,' he
corrected throatily.

'I'll still be here when you get back,' she promised.

'You'd better be,' he threatened.

When he had gone Sabina lay back against the pil-
lows, basking in Joel's love. He had told her time and
time again how much he loved her, had—What was that
strange noise? Oh lord, they had forgotten all about
Satan! Could he possibly still be under the bed?

She got out of bed to have a look, but she couldn't
see anything. It was dark under the bed, and his black
fur made it impossible for her to see anything but the
gleam of his eyes. He blinked occasionally, so at least he
was alive. They would have to get him to a vet today,
there had to be something seriously wrong with him.

Joel's smile widened as he came back into the room
to find her standing beside the bed stark naked. 'Mm,'
he took her into his arms, his lips caressing her throat
and shoulders. 'Beautiful,' he murmured, his hands
caressing.

Her breathing was ragged. 'Who was it at the door,
Joel?' She tried to think sensibly, something she found
hard to do when in his arms.

'Reporters. Our two friends from Scotland. They'd

finally decided to do a story about our being together up there. The fact that you're now Mrs Joel Brent was of much more interest to them, so they went away happy. Now how about making me happy?' he growled.

'I—I wish I could,' she said weakly. 'But it's Satan, Joel. I'm worried about him.'

He frowned. 'Good heavens, I'd forgotten about him. He's still under there?'

'Mm,' she nodded. 'I think you should get a torchlight and see if he's all right.'

'You're really that worried about him?'

'Really. He could be very ill, there's some strange noises coming from under there.'

'Okay,' Joel shrugged, going to the kitchen and coming back with a torch. He bent down to peer under the bed. 'Satan? Come on, boy. Let's—Well, I'll be damned! My God!'

Sabina was instantly at his side. 'What is it? What's wrong?'

Joel sat back. 'I don't believe it,' he said dazedly.

'Joel? Tell me!'

He handed her the torch. 'Take a look for yourself. I don't think we'll be going anywhere for a while.'

Sabina paled. 'He isn't . . .?'

'Have a look. Go on, Sabina,' he began to laugh, 'look for yourself.'

She did so, shining the torch into the corner where she knew Satan to be. Curled up beside him were three very tiny kittens, two black ones, and a black and white one. They didn't look more than a few hours old.

Sabina sat up. 'But—I—He——'

'*She*,' Joel corrected with a chuckle. 'He is a she. No wonder he—she has been acting so strangely.' He began to laugh in earnest now. 'My God, Satan is a female!'

Sabina took another look at the doting mother and

her kittens. 'Aren't they adorable?' she smiled dreamily. 'Joel, can we——'

'Yes, we can keep them,' he said indulgently. 'Then there'll be one for each of the children we plan to have.'

'Only three?' Sabina went into his arms, removing the robe he wore. 'But you told me I should have half a dozen,' she reminded him.

'Mm, why not?' His mouth claimed hers.

'I suppose we'll have to call her Satin now. I can't think of anything feminine that's in the least like Satan. Do you think——'

'Quiet, woman,' Joel growled, carrying her to the bed. 'We have work to do. It isn't easy having half a dozen children. But we'll have a hell of a time trying.'

'I love you,' she said shyly.

'Now that sort of talking I like.' He kissed her mouth, her throat, her breasts, engulfing her in his love once again.

 **ROMANCE**

Variety is the spice of romance

Each month, Mills & Boon publish new romances. New stories about people falling in love. A world of variety in romance – from the best writers in the romantic world. Choose from these titles in October.

FLASH POINT Jane Donnelly
DANGEROUS RAPTURE Sue Peters
FALCON'S PREY Penny Jordan
NO YESTERDAYS Sheila Strutt
ANOTHER LIFE Rosemary Carter
UNTAMED WITCH Patricia Lake
SHADOWED REUNION Lillian Cheatham
DARK ENIGMA Rebecca Stratton
THE STORMS OF SPRING Sandra Field
DAUGHTER OF THE MISTY GORGES
Essie Summers

On sale where you buy paperbacks. If you require further information or have any difficulty obtaining them, write to : Mills & Boon Reader Service, PO Box 236, Thornton Road, Croydon, Surrey CR9 3RU, England.

Mills & Boon
the rose of romance